CU01461225

THE
WOMAN IN
WHITE

E.M. McCONNELL

Copyright © 2024 by E.M. McConnell

All rights reserved. No part of this publication may be reproduced or transmitted in any form or by any means, mechanical or electronic, including photocopying or recording, or by any information storage and retrieval system, or transmitted by email, without permission in writing by the author. Reviewers may quote brief passages in reviews.

Cover Design by Ruth Anna Evans

This book has some scenes and themes of a dark nature. Please consult the final page for a detailed list of content warnings.

"Sometimes human places create inhuman monsters."

Stephen King

OTHER WORKS

CONTENTS

THE WOMAN IN WHITE

I am a monster
Ripped apart
Born from blood
They made me what
I am
The baying in my blood
A thousand
Black hounds
I am what they made me
Rage forged from
Bitter smoke
Acrid tears
Whispers
We all return to water
In the end
A dark blessing

EMILY: RATIONS AND ADVICE

LONDON, 1940

E mily shuffled the ration cards, trying to make sense of them. The writing always got jumbled up, and she forgot how much she had left to use. When she handed them over, she was worried because the shopkeepers looked at her in that laughing way, and she wasn't sure if they were cheating her. She never seemed to get enough for herself and the children, no matter how hard she tried. She would have to try harder. Eddie seemed to be growing like a weed.

"Emily? Em! Are you away with the fairies again?"

Emily looked up from the cards, forcing a smile. Mrs Sim was always telling her she was in a daydream. "I was just thinking about where to get these filled, Mrs Sim. I seem to get there too late for the good stuff."

Mrs Sim tutted. "You really should have got the hang of it by now, Emily. It's not like the war will stop just because you can't adapt! You need to go early, and make sure they know your face. Which shops do you use?"

Emily thought. "I use the greengrocers on Main St and the butcher here, near the factory."

Another woman joined in. She was from the floor, but Emily did not know her name. She crossed her arms over her coat and wobbled her chins as she spoke. "No, no, don't use Main. She never gives anything good out to the likes of us. Try Taylors on Green St. Or up on Market Place, that small one. They always have extra stuff. You have to do more shopping around now, you know. Did your ma not teach you anything?"

"Oh, yes, Taylors is good. I like Mrs Hampton on West. She always has a smile and a bit extra underneath, if you get my meaning." Mrs Sims winked and everyone laughed. Emily felt more and more confused. How could she do all this and work? How did they manage this?

She followed the gaggle of women out of the factory, clutching her cards closely. Their conversation moved on to the usual gossip that they liked to indulge in, of who was taking in extra work, who was getting married, who was not but should be, which always got the significant looks, and which girls were out flirting. Emily didn't engage. She didn't know enough about people, and they always seemed to move on quickly when she was there, like she was a child.

At last, they paused, looking at her with that same expression they always did, as if she had been shown up. Lacking. Again.

"We're at war, you know, Emily. You need to get better at this. You have mouths to feed."

Emily just mumbled, "Yes, Miss," quietly. They were right. There was a war on and she had to adapt, somehow. She turned her face towards home, trying to remember the names and places that they said. She didn't dare ask again.

Her evening passed in a blur of sticky hands and mending and voices, shrill and grumbling. Nonna wasn't happy with the quality of the meat and would just tut when anyone ever said, but there's a war on, ma! She just grumbled on, rocking away in the best spot by the fire, her mouth puckered and gathered together as if Emily's thread had caught a knot and pulled it all together. She kept her head bowed over her mending. The light was fading and soon they would pinch out the lamp.

Her bones were heavy with exhaustion. Not that Emily said anything about it. They were all tired. Mam looked like she had aged a decade since the beginning of the year, her shoulders bowed under the strain of keeping everyone fed and under the same roof. She looked over at the two small heads tucked in together in the corner. Before, they had their own room in their little house, back when Jim was still at home. But since he got called up, it was more sensible to stay with her parents and squeeze in wherever there was some room.

Emily sighed. "Have you heard from your Jimmy, Emily?"

Mam's sharp ears caught everything. "Not for a while, Mam. I sent a letter a week ago, maybe. I suppose he's just busy out there."

"Busy! Busy. We're busy! I bet he's busy, off playing soldier while we're hiding from the bombs that are coming. Why isn't he busy stopping that man dropping the bombs on us?"

Someone groaned. It could have been May, who had stopped by for tea. "I don't think they're out there playing soldier, Nonna. They're doing their best. Didn't you hear the Father last weekend? We've got to pray for our brave men. That's not playing!"

Nonna glared back, undeterred. "They're playing. They all call it playing. They're out there knocking up French ladies -"

"Mam!" Mam sat up straight, her mouth open. "Mind your language. There's children present!"

"Hmm. Well, they need to know, sooner or later. It's what they're all doing. We might as well say it out loud. Bunch of nonsense. They should send me over. I'll sort that midget with a 'tache out."

Everyone chuckled. Even Emily did, imagining her Nonna, armed with just her handbag and her umbrella, giving the scary man a good talking to. She had only seen him once, when she snuck in to watch a film with her sister, but she didn't forget. Emily had nightmares for weeks after about him. After the umpteenth time of her waking everyone up, Meggie had finally confessed to their sin and she wasn't allowed to go again. Emily didn't know if she minded it, really. It was strange, sitting there in the dark, with the ghostly screen in front of her. She would rather hear her sisters tell her afterwards how the story went.

Mam was watching her. Emily could feel it, her gaze a responsibility, another burden she was prepared to take on. She lifted her eyes from her mending. Mam's eyes were sad. "Did you do alright today at work, lamb?"

Emily nodded, eagerly. "I did, and the supervisor said I was doing better. And some of the women told me where to use the ration cards. It's all working out, you'll see, Mam."

Her mam smiled but it wasn't her real smile. It was the other one, when her back ached and she held sad things in her mouth that she didn't know what to say. "And did you think about what to do about Eddie and Betty?"

She couldn't help but let her temper rise. Emily put her mending down in her lap and scowled. "No, I haven't thought about it. I promised Jimmy that I would look after them. What kind of mother would I be if I sent them away?"

"It would mean you're a good mother, Emily." Mam's whisper was quiet, but delivered with enough force to make her point stick. Emily hadn't been mothering long enough to get that right. Her children either laughed or looked afraid when she tried to be strict. She hated that.

"The bombs are coming," Mam continued, leaning forward to not disturb the others, her eyes fixed on Emily's face. "They are coming. Don't let anyone tell you otherwise. The radio said that the man over there in Germany, he's moving into France soon. That's near us. You need to think about it. When your husband said look after them, he didn't mean leave them in danger. Just think about it. Alright?"

Emily had no intention of thinking about it. She didn't want them far away from her, all alone. She shivered. But she bowed her head in acknowledgement to her mam, who sighed. Mam knew that it wasn't going to happen.

Emily wondered what the bombs would be like. Only the older ones remembered being in a war before, and everyone was saying this one was different. Worse, somehow. She thought about all the people at the factories, the young women out meeting soldiers and enjoying themselves. They didn't seem to be worrying about the bombs. Maybe Mam was just worrying too much. But she thought again of the man with his angry eyes shouting at the crowd and she felt frightened again. He was a monster man. She knew that. And if he was coming, then maybe she was wrong. She couldn't fight him like her Jimmy, or Nonna could. She couldn't protect her children from monsters like they could.

She looked at her mending but had no heart to finish it. Instead, Emily crumpled her hands into it, wondering if life would ever be normal again.

Gemma: A New Place

London, Present Day

"Last box!" Zoe staggered in with it, her cheeks red with exertion. "You owe me so much wine, lady." She dropped the box and looked around, breathing heavily. "Well, this is nice!"

Gemma had to agree. It was a nice flat. They were on the fourth floor of a brand new development and probably one of the first people moving in, too. She stepped over to look out of the big window that showcased the London city skyline. It was like a work of art, with the river rushing past ribbon-like in the distance. Tearing herself away from the view, she smiled at her friend. "Have a look around. It's not big, but it's mine."

The sitting room was well sized, with the big window as a centrepiece and an open kitchen in what looked like corporation-beige at the right of it. There was a tiny hallway that opened into the communal corridor and the lift, and the archway next to the kitchen led to the bedroom, bathroom and tiny utility room. Zoe poked her head in, then squeezed past the boxes to have a look. She emerged, nodding with approval. "It's nicely sized for London, too. You did well here. Did you get priority because of your work?"

"Exactly. I'm classed as an essential worker so I was able to bid for one of the affordable rents. There's a few in here that will go for the big bucks. Probably on the top floors, where the priority lifts go. Not for the peasants like me!"

Zoe laughed, looking around. "And you're not bothered about it being on the site of the prison?"

Gemma scoffed. "No, I'm not superstitious like that. And they ripped the entire building down anyway. It's just land, now. Why, are you thinking the place will be haunted?"

Zoe shivered. "Maybe. I know the prison was haunted, anyway. I think they killed people there. I mean, they executed people there, as well as people who died there. I wouldn't have set foot in the place." She looked around the apartment again. "But this place feels fine. It feels new."

"It is new. Brand new! I agree, it doesn't feel like an old place. If there were ghosts," She paused and grinned at her friend, raising her eyebrows significantly, "No, I am not going to fall in with your woo ways, Zo. If there were, I think they died with the prison. When it was taken down."

Zoe nodded in a serious fashion, lost in thought. "I hope so. I had heard a few stories about hauntings in the prison. Wes told me about a woman who walks the corridors with keys on a chain, so she might have been staff before she died. And they said there was someone who screamed at night. That must have been scary. And there was the Woman in White, of course."

"I haven't heard of her. Who was she?"

Zoe smiled at her archly, raising her eyebrows again. "It's an interesting tale. Are you sure you want to hear it?"

"No, I do. Here, help me with this," Gemma said, as she pushed the sofa into place and pulled the cushions from the pile to put on. She unrolled the rug and put the coffee table on it. "There, the sitting room is almost complete."

Zoe threw herself down on the sofa in her usual way, heaving a delighted sigh as she landed. Gemma followed suit, in a more low-key manner, and turned to face her friend. "Who was she?"

"Well," Zoe began, in an overly dramatic fashion. She smiled. Her friend had always been like that. "The Woman in White has been named because she is dressed in a long white dress, of course, and she stalks the prison. She has really long hair, and she doesn't say anything. But if you see her, she'll stalk you for a while. You hear dripping of water everywhere you go, or she floods a room with water and emerges out of it, Wes said. She's pretty scary. They think she was a prisoner who died there, or was hanged there, maybe, and she stays within the walls, walking about."

"Water? Why water? There isn't much in the way of water by here, is there?"

"Nobody knows. But she clearly likes the stuff. I don't think she's tried to kill anyone with it yet, but I suppose it would be hard to be diagnosed with a watery death if a ghost does it. Oh, she did show herself to the prisoners sometimes, too. Not as often. Maybe she likes to haunt men."

Gemma pursed her lips. "Well, she doesn't sound that bad to me. Leaky tap noises is hardly Ghostbusters, is it? Are you sure they're not just scaring themselves silly with ghost stories?"

Zoe shrugged with one shoulder, letting it rise and then fall. It was a studied gesture, one that she used a lot. "I have no idea. I don't think Wes ever saw her, or if he did, he never mentioned it to me, but he certainly believed in her. He seemed to think she was like some kind of prison mascot. Once you got successful in the prison; then you saw her. Obviously, they shut it down before he got his chance."

"Where's he been sent to now? He moved again recently, didn't he?"

"He's gone to Belmarsh, but he doesn't like it much. He said it's different locking up the men, they're more aggressive. And he has to take a couple of buses to get to work now. He could have gone to another women's prison but they're all out of London. He didn't want to shift and start again. But now, he's not sure."

Gemma stayed quiet. She suspected that if Zoe had said she would go with him, he would happily start again, but Gemma wasn't going to tell her that, selfishly. She wanted to keep her friend near. It was hard to make new friends at her age, especially with her shifts. It was better for Zo to stay in London, anyway. There was more opportunity to be had.

Zoe looked out at the window, and the advancing sun, and then back at the boxes. "We need to get some of these unpacked or you'll be sleeping in a pigsty. How about, we do some boxes, you order a takeaway, WITH WINE, and then we christen the place with a movie?"

Gemma smiled. "That sounds good. But no scary films. Something funny!" Zoe winked. "Deal."

Together they shifted boxes and unpacked in the dying light as the sun blanketed the skyline with golden light. It really was beautiful. Zoe sighed, hands on her hips, as she looked out. "I think that view is worth a million squids, you know. I bet it's even better in the penthouses. You'll have to engineer a meeting with one of the rich people and get yourself in there to see how much nicer it is."

"What, and then come back here and feel disappointed? Not on your nelly, woman. I'm sticking with what I've got!"

"Yeah, I would, too. You did well with this."

Zoe stood looking out of the window again as Gemma ordered the takeaway and wine, feeling glad that they delivered here. Some companies were funny about delivering to new builds, or they weren't on the system yet. But it all went smoothly. That job done, she joined her at the window, tucking her phone into her back jeans pocket.

Neither noticed the slight decrease in temperature, or the tap in the kitchen starting to drip.

Emily:
Imminent Raids

They finished their shift early that day, as the manager had been given word of an imminent raid. The chap who delivered the message looked important and official, very pleased with himself. Emily wondered if he would look so pleased if the bombs actually started to fall. She looked up to the sky, just in case, wondering if you would see them. Would you hear them? She thought Nonna had said that you know when it's happening, but she couldn't remember why. There were no bombs or planes, though, just the usual clouds.

She hurried onwards, not wanting to try the buses. They were unreliable when it wasn't rush hour now, but she preferred to walk. It was nice to get some fresh air. The air in the factory was stifled with cigarettes and gossip. It made her cough and wheeze. She knew it made them laugh, that she looked like she wasn't fit to work there, but she ignored them. It wasn't the work. It was the way they made it difficult to be there.

It was still quiet, which was nice. There were some people going to the different shops, more coming back

out with empty bags than full, though. The ones that
got stuff tended to hide it, so people didn't look
funny at them. Everyone was hungry now. If they
saw someone had more than everyone else, they'd
probably get angry. Emily was glad she didn't have
to deal with the ration books today. It made her head
hurt. All she had to do was go back, see Mam, and
tend to the children. That was enough.

Hurrying across the road, she dodged two bicycles
that flew through hell for leather as if the hounds
from hell were after them. She reached the kerb
safely and marched on as fast as she could. Mam
would be waiting and she looked tired this morning.
The last thing Mam needed was taking on two small
children as well, but she said she would manage, just
as always. Emily hoped she wouldn't bring up the
evacuation thing again. After the first time, and so
many children had left, Emily wondered if she had
made a mistake keeping hers near, but the bombs
did not fall, and the children were slowly brought
back. Now it was being talked about again.

Could she not just pretend it wasn't happening and
let her two babies just carry on as they were? Emily
didn't know. It was hard making all the decisions.
Normally, Jimmy made the decisions, but he was
a long way away. Mam had mentioned France yes-
terday and that the bad man was nearly in France.
Emily hoped Jimmy wasn't in France.

Two of the ARP girls skated past, hair blowing in
the wind. They were fast on their wheels, bag at their
hip, as they flew through the streets. They looked free.
Emily wished that she had an important job like that.

But they had taken one look at her and assigned her to a factory. Perhaps they knew best.

Emily sighed and turned away. In the next road there was a pub with the door opening, and a group spilling out. There were two men in uniform, cigarettes in their mouths, holding pretty ladies by the waist. They were laughing and smiling, eyes sparkling. They looked as if there was no war on at all. Just as if there was only joy and fun in the world.

Someone shoved her in the back, making her gasp and turn round. It was Mrs Sim, her face purple with horror. "Emily, what are you doing, loitering like that? Do you want one of those soldiers thinking you're an easy woman? Get moving and get home before your parents find out what you're up to!"

Flustered, Emily put her head down and scuttled off, her face growing red. What did Mrs Sim mean? What was she doing wrong, apart from daydreaming? She was only standing there. Were the soldiers really dangerous? Her Jimmy was a soldier, and he wasn't dangerous. Emily didn't understand, and she hated that. People just didn't speak clearly.

She didn't stop once, not looking around her, but just hurrying through the streets, eager to get back. Home was nice. Home was safe. She would get home.

Mam met her at the door, her tired face looking surprised. "We were let out early. They said the bombs were coming."

Emily stepped inside, greeting the children and turning to her mending. Her mam shut the door carefully. "Well, if there's bombs, we'll have to make the best of it. We know what to do." The children were wide-eyed, listening. Mam swatted at Betty. "You two mind your ears or you'll hear things you needn't hear. Betty, help your mam. Eddie, you can help me." The children rose obediently to help, Betty settling comfortably into Emily's lap. She smelled of flour and washing. Emily breathed it in, wishing she could just stay there and not go out to the factory again.

Mam was moving about in her practised manner, Eddie moving with her as if he were her shadow. The sun lit up the greys in her hair. She was getting older. Emily wondered what she would look like when she was that age. Would Eddie move out and find a wife, and would Betty stay at her side? Or would she grow old with Jimmy alone in their little house? Emily stirred herself from her daydream. Betty had fallen asleep against her chest. Emily shifted her daughter so she would be more comfortable.

"Ma Olsen from down the road has taken ill again, so I'll need to pick up some of her laundry. You can run down for it later. I heard that John who lives over the way has some extra vegetables going spare. I'll see if I can get some potatoes for a stew. We're always short of those. I might set Jimmy to growing an allotment outside, if you don't end up sending him to the country. And I haven't forgotten about it so don't think I have."

Mam gave her a stern look. "And don't let that baby sleep too long on you. She'll get used to it and be up all night wailing. Some of us need to work tomorrow." Her gaze softened. "What will you do with finishing early today, will you have to make the time up?"

"Yes, Mam. I'll stay later tomorrow and Friday to collect my full wages. Mrs Sand said that would be alright.

She was pleased with my work today. She said I'm doing well."

Emily felt warm inside when her mam beamed. It was nice to make her proud. "Well done, Emily. I'm pleased. You snuggle that baby for a minute. They're only young once, right? We're going to go see about those vegetables."

She slipped out of the door with Eddie holding her hand, and Emily rested her head back on Betty's head. It would all be fine. The war would be done with soon and everything would be normal. Everyone would be just fine.

GEMMA: JUST SEEING THINGS. NOT A PROBLEM

The doors hissed shut behind her as Gemma jumped on her new train to go home. She would never tire of it, just one tube, door to door. Well, practically door to door. A walk on either side was fine, welcome, even, after a busy shift. It gave her time to decompress. But she found that she hardly had to settle on the tube before the quiet voice announced her spot and tipped her out again for her short walk home. Home.

She knew she was lucky to have it, lucky to land a new apartment in London, of all places, but it was more than that. She was lucky to have a place that was hers, nobody else's. Nobody could take it; nobody could snatch it from her hands at their whim. That, too, was something she would never tire of.

It was a short walk with headphones before her building was in sight, and she fumbled for her keys. The sun was fading and that always made her cautious. In the rosy light of evening, she unlocked the main door, striding to the lift. She did not want to take the stairs. It was only four flights, but no. There was a lift, she probably paid for the lift, so she was using the lift.

Her apartment was welcoming, warm, and quiet. She dropped her keys in the bowl that she was given when she moved in, a gift from her very highly organised uncle who probably never lost anything, especially not essential items. Not like she did.

The sun lit up the floor like a flame as it set over London, and she sighed as she watched. It really was beautiful. A quiet but insistent drip wormed its way into her ears, and she looked over at the kitchen. Her tap was dripping, one drop forming slowly before descending into the sink. Gemma frowned. That sort of sound would drive her mad before long. She tightened the tap, quelling the flow, and glanced around her apartment. It was tidy, just as she left it, but something struck her as different.

She stared for a moment, pondering, and then shook her head. She headed for the shower instead, eager to get rid of the hospital stink that clung to her clothes.

It was dark when she returned, the window now a reflection of the soft lamp next to the sofa. It was as if someone had muffled the outside with darkness, even in the city that never slept. But she had lived in London long enough not to notice the noise and traffic, or the bustle. Being four floors up helped, too. It was quiet, up so high. And either the home builders had done a great job with soundproofing, or not many had moved in yet; it was still quiet, echoing in the corridors as she arrived and left. It would be nice if they were a bit of a community. Perhaps she should set up a get-together, organise a building event or something. But that took planning, and she had a busy job. Perhaps not.

The hours of the evening stretched out in front of her like a void. It was hard to be alone sometimes; all the tasks still needed to be done, but there would never be a surprise when you found out that someone had done them already, like a dinner already in the oven, or that morning's washing up draining next to the sink. It was why she rarely cooked at night. It was another task, another chore that she couldn't take joy in, as she couldn't share it with someone. Perhaps she should get a cat to share her news with. But it was perhaps not fair to keep a cat inside all the time.

She settled on the sofa, wriggling the fatigue out of her feet and reaching for her blanket. She could fill the void with something funny on television, and still the quiet for a while.

It was dark. Very dark. Gemma blinked and stared, trying to see past the end of her nose, trying to make sense of the shapes that looked so different in the night. How had she fallen asleep on the sofa? It hadn't even been particularly difficult, the work this week. It was cold, too. Very cold. She pulled the blanket closer, wondering what time it might be. Should she just go and get into bed?

And there was that noise again. Drip, drip, drip. Her eyes cut to the kitchen, narrowing on the tap. How was it dripping again? She was sure she had tightened it. She would have to report that to the landlord and ask them to look at it.

It really was cold. She shivered and sat up, wondering if there was a sudden low pressure front arriving up the river. And then, she froze. The floor was like ice, solid, as if it were a river that had ceased to flow, and let the wind wither it into hardened ice. The cold seeped in even through her socks, making her bones hurt. But her attention was not on the floor, even as it stole the heat from the soles of her feet, her ankles, and her calves.

She was not alone. In the corner of the room, right by the window, there was a woman, face indistinct, dressed in a white gown. And she was staring right at her. She was staring, right at her. She was staring. Gemma could feel her eyes. Her eyes, that she could not see, but she could feel. Staring.

Her scream died in her throat. Her eyes widened, filled with fear, as the cold froze her blood. Tears spilled from her eyes as she blinked, her heart pounding. And then, the figure began to move, jerking into position, stepping towards her...

Gemma awoke with a start, clutching her blanket, her heart screaming in her chest. It was fine. It was just a bloody horrible dream. Scrambling to her feet, she ran to her bedroom, not looking up, not looking back. But she felt eyes on her back as she ran, stifling sobs that lodged in her chest.

It was just a nightmare. It's totally normal to run to your room. Everything was fine. Her room looked normal, untouched, and she sighed with relief as she shut the door with her foot and leapt into bed, still clutching her blanket. It was fine. She was fine. It was a bad dream. It was just a bad dream.

EMILY: ATTACKED

Dusk had crept in before they were let loose that evening, despite them looking hopefully over every thirty minutes since the finish bell went at 4.30 as usual. Emily wished she had been lazy and opted for the lower wages, but she could do with not skimping this week. Jimmy needed new shoes and she wanted to get something for Nonna's chest, as she was coughing now the spring rains had set in. Emily hoped it would be a better summer, and the bombs wouldn't come. If they stayed away, maybe it would be alright. Surely, the planes had enough else to do, anyway.

Her heels clicked smartly on the pavement. They weren't really heels, not like the shoes the fancy ladies wore, but she liked hearing them anyway. They were good enough for her, and her Jimmy always said he liked seeing her dressed up smart. Emily sighed as she walked, bag clutched tightly to her chest.

It felt a bit different after dark, with the alleyways that she couldn't see down and the people being more watchful. But everyone left her alone. The pub that she had seen the other day was brightly lit with warm orange light, but the door was shut. Perhaps they didn't need to invite more people in. It was busy enough already. It was Friday and people had wages to spend. Emily clutched her own wages tighter still to her chest.

She needed to get home. Safely. She walked faster, turning onto the main street and leaving the pub at her back. The street was quiet, of course. The shops were all closed and everyone was busy at their business. Emily hummed to herself as she walked, letting her feet be the beat. She wondered if May would visit and bring her new records to listen to this weekend. Sometimes she did, if she found what she wanted at the record store. It was always exciting. Everyone would gather round to listen, Nonna pretending she wasn't having anything to do with all that new-fangled nonsense, even as her feet tapped away on the floor. Perhaps May would even bring her new man and they would dance.

Emily smiled, turning the corner. It wasn't far now. She crossed the road, deciding to take the shortcut behind the warehouse and cross the railway tracks. It was never used at this time, and it would cut a good ten minutes off her time. Mam would have her dinner ready on the stove, but she could take a minute to see the children before they went to bed. Perhaps she could take them out for a walk tomorrow if it wasn't too wet, and even get Eddie fitted for his new shoes. She skipped slightly, humming.

It might not be ladylike to go out to work, although they had to during wartime, but Emily found she liked doing it, liked being able to provide for her children, and not have to try and save from her pin money. It was hers to do with as she saw fit. It made her feel responsible. Adult, even.

The warehouse was dark and silent, but the road behind it was wide. On one side were bushes and the embankment, which was heavily overgrown. She could see the road in the distance, with its lights and a few cars. *Nearly home. Nearly home.*

Shadows moved as two men walked from the doors of the warehouse. Emily kept walking, moving a little further away, aiming for the road.

But they kept walking, getting closer. Emily clutched her bag a little closer. She would get Eddie's shoes, and maybe a nice ribbon for Betty's hair. Betty would like that. Maybe her Jimmy had sent a letter. Maybe it was sitting on the mantelpiece, waiting for her. Emily nodded to herself, squeezing her bag, walking a bit faster.

The men began to catch up with her, the shadows, walking beside her, clicking in time with her shoes, *oh, she wished she had not worn these shoes,* and just walking, walking like hunting cats. Emily had watched the cats hunt in the yard, by the river, their eyes on their prey, moving slowly, positioning, wanting.

This was those men. They were man-cats.

Emily had to walk faster. The road was in sight. Her Jimmy's letter was in sight. She just had to get home. It wasn't far.

The cats cut off her path, with wide smiles and glinting eyes. "Hi, beautiful! Where are you headed?" "Can we walk you home? It's not safe around here, you know."

One on each side, arms reaching in, slowing her down.

"What's your name?" "Hey, it's nice to be nice, why not say hello?"

The road. Emily had her eyes on the road. It was so close

"I'm just going home. I've finished work and my Mam is expecting me." Emily tried to move, feeling the arms tighten. "I just need to go-"

"What's the hurry?" "There's no need to be rude, you know. What's your name?"

No. Do not tell them your name. "I just really need to get home. Thank you, though," Emily tried to extricate her arms and move away. The arms held fast. Fear rose.

"You really shouldn't be out on your own. There are all sorts about." "Being out this late is really asking for trouble." They laughed together, ignoring her. She struggled. "I'll be home in a moment. Please?"

Maybe her begging was an invitation. They were wild cats, mauling, ripping, howling. Feral cats in the dark, glorying in the hunt. And as they gloried, Emily cried.

GEMMA: WATERLOGGED

The bar was loud, loaded with cheap perfume and cheap beer, just the way the patrons liked it. Normally, she liked it, too. Today, she was out of sync, out of sorts, out of step.

She step-floated her way to where her friends were, waving, sitting down, letting herself be absorbed in the chatter, the pull of embraces and smiles and greetings. She did enough to not stand out. To all but Zoe, of course, who watched and smiled, yet tilted her head ever so slightly, as she took in the fact that Bestie was actually not okay.

Obviously, Zoe didn't dive right in, but left it to settle, for conversation to move on, and for people to go for more drinks, before she leaned in. "You look like shit, Gem. What's occurring?"

Gemma picked up her drink, raising it in a mock salute. "I've not been sleeping well. I'm getting haggard." Her tone was light, teasing.

Zoe smiled, eyes not leaving her friend's face. "Is it work? You haven't had any more of those things, have you -"

"Oh, no, nothing like that. Work has been a bit hectic with the upcoming promotion and I've had some tough shifts, but I don't think it's going to send me off sick or anything. And no, I've not had any more letters. I think the move put paid to that, thankfully."

Gemma kept her tone light, although she felt her voice wobble a bit. The letters had frightened her: anonymous, knowing, and dark. She still didn't know who had sent them, who had said that they were out there watching her, wanting her from afar. Hopefully, it was just a prank that ended now she had moved again without leaving a forwarding address.

"And how's Wes doing? Is he settling in at the new place?"

Zoe smiled, letting her change the subject. "He's doing alright. He's working late this week, but he seems to be getting there now. He said it took a bit longer to get a routine with the men, but he prefers the lack of flirting. Some of the women would get a bit rude, sometimes. You know. Flirtatious. Pushy."

Zoe leaned forward, her face bright. "I've got some other news for you, too. But I'll tell you later. When everyone's gone." She withdrew, leaving the mystery for Gemma to untangle, as their friends returned.

Fliss was loud, waving her drink about as she related funny stories about work to Brian and Grey, and Zoe gently teased Ben, who sat at the edge of the group, rarely joining in as usual. Gemma settled and relaxed, absorbing the chatter, the mirth, and the smiles. Life might not be perfect, but it was good. She had her new place, she was safe there, she was going to be promoted, and she had her friends. That was more than most. It would all be just fine.

Her apartment was waiting with a warm glow thanks to all the lamps on a timer. Murmuring quiet thanks to her dad

who had programmed them for her, Gemma collapsed into her couch. Her body was exhausted: the long shifts always took their toll physically but sometimes the mental exhaustion was even worse.

She barely had the energy to watch TV, let alone do something productive with her evening. Picking up her phone, she shot Zoe back a quick message and scrolled through her social media feed. There were perfectly edited photos of smiling women, arms wrapped around reluctant boyfriends, and the usual photos of food. A typical weekend, then. She didn't miss it. Gemma's most recent ex was one for the staged photo, and she hated seeing her face twisted into a grimace, plastered up all over the place. She was well out of that, too.

There was movement just at the edge of her peripheral vision, and Gemma turned quickly to look. The kitchen was empty. She had to have been imagining it. It was just an odd light or something, maybe. Gemma stared hard at the wall, then returned to her phone. Her heart was racing. There was nothing to worry about. Eyes played tricks on you all the time. It was fine.

Losing her appetite for the mindless scrolling, she put the phone away. She could cook something, that would be productive. Maybe call her dad. He would like that, Dad always had time to talk. Gemma could do both at once, and that kept the silence away as she cooked.

This was the plan. She started to bustle about in the kitchen, setting her phone against the stand and hitting the call button. As her dad's booming voice filled the room, she relaxed.

"Hey, munchkin! I wasn't expecting to speak to you today. Is everything alright?"

"Hi, dad. It's great. I just wanted to check in with you. How are you doing?"

His face loomed into the screen, as if he needed to poke his face right into his phone to call. Gemma stifled a laugh.

"Everything is good, munchkin. I've got a week off coming up, so if you need anything doing, let me know. And I've got some post here for you. Hang on," he said, putting the phone down with a clatter. The familiar fear gripped her, holding her chest in a vice. Her movements were deliberate and careful as she waited. It was fine. There wouldn't be a letter. He reappeared with envelopes in his hand, all white and brown. "Just bills, I think, they're all typed addresses. Do you need me to drop them off quick for you or wait?"

Just bills. There was no need to worry. She was over-re-acting, or catastrophising, as she would say to her patients. Always jumping to the worst conclusion wasn't a healthy approach. Gemma knew that, but she couldn't help doing it. "No, just bring them when you come. Can you look at the tap, actually? It keeps leaking. And the curtain rails in the bedrooms haven't been put up yet. Is that OK?"

He beamed, his grin wide. "Leave that for me. You know I like to be useful! Now, I don't want to keep you, Gem. And my show's on in a bit. I'll talk to you soon, yeah?"

Of course. Of course, it was that time. With a pang, Gemma agreed, smiling her farewells and blowing a kiss to his hurried departure, the screen going dark. She did wish he would keep her, sometimes, instead of rushing off. But he had his own life, too. It wasn't his fault that she was lonely.

She cooked hurriedly, just making the pasta and adding a pesto rather than going to any real effort, and eating it standing up at the counter rather than at the table. She let the TV blare into the silence, filling the empty space where a person should be. It was almost enough, really. Almost.

It wasn't until there was a lull in the programme that she heard the noise again, the drip, drip of the tap. She mustn't have tightened it properly earlier when she cooked. Frustrated, she went to switch it off. As she turned back towards the sofa, she saw water slowly pooling in the doorway of the bathroom, pushing its way out in a dark shadow of a curve, filling the space. That was all she needed right now. Fucking brilliant.

Stifling a curse, she walked closer to get the mop. There was clearly a problem with the waterworks in this place. She would have to check with the other occupants. The mop was exactly where she had left it, which was a relief. Too often, things seemed to move around, just like in her last place. Gripping the handle with determination, she emerged from the cupboard and blinked, confused. The floor was bone-dry.

She frowned, stepping into the bathroom and switching the light on. No water. She felt a shiver of fear between her shoulder blades and stepped back quickly towards the safe light of the lamps. It was a trick of the light, that was all. Nothing to worry about. Nothing at all.

Gemma woke with a start, pulling her quilt closer to her. This was happening too often, waking up when it got too cold. She needed to get another blanket. But her heart was pounding in her chest as she shivered. This wasn't the heating, and it wasn't freak cold spells in the middle of the night. Her breath came out in clouds of smoke and ice frosted on the inside of the windows. Her breath came in gasps as she shivered, her blood cooling, sweat rolling down her back. Cold sweat. The cold sweat of terror. It was dark but the moon rose, bringing a cold white light with it. It reflected on the water that filled her room, that rose slowly, dark water that boiled and rose, flooding her room.

Her bed was a boat, a safe space that she clung to as the water lapped at her bed. Gemma thought no more of taps or pipes. She remembered what her friend had said. The Woman in White rose out of water...

Her eyes scanned the water that was there, impossibly, almost at her quilt, a dark river in her room. And then she saw a head break from the waters, blonde hair in the dark black, tearing the surface, her face, her face gnawed by water, by fish, white, her withered mouth opening, her arms swathed in white lifting, as she rose in the night.

Gemma found her voice and screamed, and screamed, and screamed.

Nobody came, as she threw herself back against her bed, quilt clutched to her chest, and the thing came nearer, dripping dank water from her hair, plastered close to her head, her eyes just dark holes of emptiness, unblinking. Gemma screamed as it stared, eyes close to hers, mouth open, eyes unblinking. The Woman in White was real, and it was haunting her.

EMILY: MAN-CAT-DEVILS

"Emily, it's time for work; you have to wake up."

The words sliced through her sleep, her unconsciousness. Emily did not want to wake up. But work. She had to work. If she didn't work, Mrs Sands would not hire her as much. She had to get up. She swung her legs out of the bed, arms blindly searching for her clothes.

"Emily."

The word hammered into her brain. She ignored it. She had to go to work. She stood, joints aching. She was so tired. "I've got to go to work, Mam. I'll see you after work." She did not stop to get food or to speak to her babies, who were still snuggled in their cots. She had to go to work.

She could hear murmuring around her, and eyes. Eyes. Watching.

"Well, at least they didn't take her wages."

"Devils, the lot of them."

Emily ignored it, keeping her eyes forward. She was going to the factory for her shift. There was value in that. The door shut quietly behind her. She sagged in relief. She had the walk to be herself for a while. There would be no cats out at this time, no eyes that were looking at her. Devils, Nonna had said. Were they devils or were they cats?

Work passed. Nobody asked her about the cats, about the scratches that she was sure everyone could see. Mam had assured her that nobody could see, that she would be fine, but it felt like they were shouting out as loud as they could.

Look at me, look what the cats did!

Devils. Devil cats.

Emily kept her head down and worked hard, shaking her head when some of the women offered her a tea at the break. Some studied her curiously, but they shrugged and went back to it.

Devils or cats? It was all Emily could think about, about the attack, about the bombs. The bombs were going to fall. She knew it. The man with the angry eyes was coming. Did he send the devil cats? Maybe that's how he planned to win the war. By breaking women. Sending cats to hunt them. Man-cats. Devil-cats.

Days passed and her Mam stopped asking, but her eyes were worried, strained. Emily's children cried again at night. They cried for her because the devil cats had taken her soul away. No, put something in her that was taking her soul. Emily knew it. They'd left a demon behind. A demon devil-cat like them.

It wasn't long before Mam and Nonna realised, too, although they didn't think it was a demon cat. They just whispered about a problem, and how to get rid of it fast. Mam arranged an appointment with a lady who sometimes did her laundry with Mrs Olsen, and she knew about these things. They would go together later. Nonna was being kind and said she would look after the children. Nonna looked more cheerful after that, knowing that the problem would be solved.

The woman lived in a very neat house on a nice road, with a freshly chalked doorstep and clean net curtains at the window. They were shown straight into the kitchen, and she pulled a jar of salve out of the oven. She passed it to Emily, giving her brief instructions of what to do with it. It smelled like mint and something like soap.

Emily complied, although she did not believe it would work. It didn't matter. Things like this worked on real babies, as they had soft, fragile bones and skin. Demon Cat babies were strong and hard and could rip their way out of soft bodies if they wanted to.

The pain started quickly, which Mam was pleased about. She handled Emily like a child, like she wasn't changing, like she wasn't a problem. It made Emily want to cry. "You take a day tomorrow, alright? I'll tell someone to tell Mrs Sands. You have a rest. Everything will be just fine."

Emily nodded, enjoying her mother's happiness, even knowing that it would not be. Mam didn't know. It wasn't her fault.

Emily watched the sky for the bombs that were coming. Would there be one with her name on it? That would be nice. Something to take the pain away. But she did not let that thought slip from her mouth. Instead, Emily fed it to the cat demon that ranged around in her womb, sharpening its claws. It grew fat on fear and blood. It was grown in blood, and it would be born in blood. And soon.

GEMMA: I'M IN DANGER

Her hands wouldn't stop shaking. She was functioning, barely, at work, but each time Gemma had a quiet moment she returned to the night before. Could she have been hallucinating? She can't have been. She was awake. She saw it with her own eyes.

But this morning the floor was dry. There was no sign of the flood, or the thing that rose out of the floorboards. Her hair stood on end again. It wasn't like she could tell anyone, either. Who would believe it? Her manager would just think she was having a nervous breakdown again, and send her right off to therapy, if she wasn't thrown right into the lock-down ward. Her dad would only worry.

Zoe's face popped into her mind. She was the one who told her about the Woman in White. What if she spoke to her? Wes could confirm what the ghost looked like, maybe. He wouldn't disbelieve her, not if he believed in ghosts. And that would mean she wouldn't have to go home so early, either.

Dread settled in her stomach. She could put it off, but she would have to go home. She had only just moved in, she couldn't go back to her dad, he had no room for her and what could she say, anyway?

Oh, I gave up my great new apartment because I keep seeing things that aren't there, but might be there, and I'm shitting myself about going back alone? He would get that line between his eyes when he was worried and start muttering about seeing the doctor. She was not doing that again.

An hour to go. She would do some paperwork, pretend she had a headache, and hole up in a corner. Gathering her files, Gemma did just that, moving to a corner and trying very hard not to think about the night before. And its face. Especially not its face.

The house was homely, warm, and alive. Gemma felt it as she arrived, approaching the door, seeing shapes move about in the window. Was it the presence of love that did it? Zoe and Wes had been close since school, probably, and then eventually moved in together. They had it, whatever 'it' was. They made a house that could have been shabby look perfect. As she walked in, Wes turned and greeted her warmly, giving her a big squeeze. Ben waved from the table, where he was looking over papers. He was wearing glasses, which suited him. He looked quite cute.

Gemma nodded to Ben as she looked around for Zo. Gemma needed the tempest, her best friend, so she could regulate somehow. The lights were all blazing, and Wes was commanding the stove, saucepans bubbling away. She shuddered when she saw the water ripple. She had to get a fix on that before she developed hydrophobia or something. But really, wouldn't anyone start being afraid of water when their apartment was being flooded and swamp ghosts were rising up to stare at you?

The saucepan rippled in response, bumping up its lid, and Gemma shivered again. It was everywhere, water. She needed to get a grip. And fast.

Ben was busy with the papers, his pen scratching away as he took notes. She sat down quietly, not wanting to disturb whatever it was he was writing. Or whatever he was working out. He looked up for a moment and nodded in an absent manner before retuning to his papers.

Gemma took a moment to study him. He wasn't the type she normally went for, but she could see the draw, the quiet efficiency, the calm. There was something to be said for that. But perhaps it was her current situation talking. Trauma overtook all, of course. She knew that better than anyone: from her job as a psych nurse and from having her breakdown. There was nothing like getting a taste for theoretical perspectives when your world was being shredded to shit.

Zoe danced in, snugly warm in a huge, oversized purple sweater and a black stretchy skirt. She slid past the table, kissed Wes, who smiled as he cooked, and then came back to the table, deftly grabbing the open wine bottle as she went. She put it in front of Gemma, gesturing to the glass. "Drink, and tell."

She did drink. She picked up the glass, took a big gulp, and set it down. Zoe was still standing, glass in hand, waiting. Gemma barely tasted it but felt the pleasant burn in her stomach. It was time to just spit the words out.

"I'm being haunted by the Woman in White."

Zoe froze, falling into a chair as if her legs had given away. The pan that Wes was using clattered against the hob, and then there was a click as he turned off the heat, turning towards her, his eyes distraught. Even Ben looked up over his glasses, eyebrows furrowed, pen hovering, as he processed the words. Wes joined them at the table.

"Tell me everything that's happened."

His tone wasn't his normal Wes tone. His normal Wes tone was in harmony with Zoe, as she ordered, he agreed. This time he was in charge, his words clipped, his brain in Protect Mode. Zoe didn't interfere, looking to him as the leader. So Gemma looked right back at him. The leader.

"It's been since I moved in, I think. I've heard the taps dripping, even when I tighten them. The floor floods and then disappears again. I've seen her in the corner, staring at me. Stuff keeps being moved about. And last night my entire bedroom floor flooded and she rose up through the floor, staring at me. I'm really scared, and I don't know what to do."

They all stared at her. Ben was holding his pen in a funny way, poised awkwardly between his fingers, as if it would drop at any moment. Zo was about to cry, or fight. It was about even based on that expression. But Wes, Wes, believed her. His eyes didn't waver, he didn't twitch or fidget. He just stared, his eyes full of concern.

"Do you need to stay here tonight?"

That was his first thought, God love him. His first thought was her safety. It wasn't often that she was jealous of her best friend having a significant other, but today she was. Not in the jealous sense of wanting him for herself. Just wishing that she had experienced one like that. Just once.

Wes was still waiting for her to answer. Gemma gulped, and thought. But it was clear. "I can't, Wes. I'm sorry. I would like to, and I am scared, but I can't just abandon my apartment. If I stay here, what if it brings her here? I can't risk it. But I am afraid, I won't deny it."

Wes took a moment to nod, his thoughts far away. "Alright, we'll make a plan for that. And is she haunting anyone else in the building, or just you?"

That brought Zoe out of her silence. "What the fuck, Wes? It's not like she's going to go and ask complete strangers if they're being haunted!"

Wes just regarded her with his new look, as if he was about to finish someone off on Mortal Kombat. He was all about it. "But they might have mentioned the plumbing thing. You would be surprised at how much people bond over stuff like that."

"I don't know, but I can ask around. Do you think it's definitely her? The Woman in White?" Her eyes cut to Ben, who was listening, his eyes and ears open. Wide open. She could understand it to an extent, but perhaps he could have looked a bit less fascinated. It's not like it was a TV show that they were discussing.

Wes shrugged. "It's on the grounds of the old prison and she's acting in the same way as before. I think it stands to reason that it's her."

"So what do we do, Wes? Gem can't live with a ghost!"

His hand went out, finding Zoe's arm, and squeezing it, and retreating again.

"No, she can't. So, we're going to live with her."

That was not expected. Gemma put her hands up, and shook her head. This was not going to happen. Wes stood up, striding up and down in the small kitchen. "What if, me and Ben stay at your house until we find out some more? We can take turns. Then you're not alone."

"And me," Zoe interjected, putting her hand on Gemma's arm. "I can stay with her too."

Wes turned and shook his head. "No."

Zoe subsided instantly, which wasn't like her. What was going on? Gemma felt resentment creeping up. They were making decisions for her, deciding about her. No. She wasn't having this.

"Wes, with all respect, and I appreciate the offer, but I don't want to have men in my flat. Where will you even sleep? How are you going to protect me if she comes into my room at night? We need a better solution."

Ben cleared his throat quietly. "I don't mind sleeping on the floor, if you like, Gemma. But I understand. I wonder if there's another way to get round this problem." He hesitated for a moment as all the eyes wheeled onto him.

"Er, I mean I am not an expert on ghosts, but we could do some research on this person, this, er, haunting, and find out what she does. We could always find a medium or clairvoyant to try and communicate with it. Would an exorcism work?"

Those were good suggestions, delivered in a calm manner. Despite her fear and stress, Gemma was impressed. Zoe leaned forward, enthused. "That's a great idea. I know of a clairvoyant, I can ask her to come to your house, Gem. I don't know where we would get an exorcism though. Does anyone even do them anymore?"

"Catholic priests do," Wes replied absently. He was thinking hard. He had that look on his face, the same one as when he was absorbed at the table planning his D and D campaigns. But this time she didn't tease him for it. She was glad he was there. "That's a good idea, though, Ben, all of it, really. I'm wondering if I can get in touch with some of the old-timers from Holloway, and see if they know about who she's haunted in the past. It gives us something to go on, anyway."

He looked at Gemma. "Are you sure you don't want someone there with you? Or a dog? I can ask my ma if she'll let me take hers?"

Gemma forced the laugh back. She didn't think that Wes' ma had the kind of dog that could protect her from a water-logged ghost, somehow. "No, don't ask her, Wes. I'd rather less people knew about it. But thanks, it's a good offer. I'll just have to handle the ghost. Pour salt around my bed or something."

She meant it as a joke, weak as it was, but Zoe took it seriously. She jumped up and fished about in her cupboard. "Here, have some extra. Throw it at her face if she comes near. Maybe it'll work like it does on slugs!"

Gemma took the salt gratefully. Maybe it did work like that! Longingly, she looked around the room, wishing she could stay there. Wishing she had a plan. Her flat was waiting for her, in the dark, and she was afraid.

Zoe was afraid too, her hands reaching out to ask her to stay. "Are you working tomorrow? Do you want to come here, after? Wes can do your tea. And we can organise the clairvoyant. Yes?"

She nodded, not wanting to say something and get all choked up. She was lucky to have a friend like Zo. One in a million. Ben pushed his glasses back up his nose, looking awkward. "I'm going to do some research into ghosts, and see if I can find anything out about her. Shall I, er, come tomorrow, too?"

His eagerness was quite endearing, like he was a lost puppy. Zoe smiled to herself. "Yes, Ben, you can come too. We'll sort this out together, right? We're the A-Team."

Wes put his arm around her. "You're not alone, Gem. We'll sort this out somehow. I promise."

EMILY:
UNRAVELLING

I t was hard to fill her days. As soon as Emily started showing she had to leave the factory, amidst congratulations and wide smiles.

"That's one in the eye for Hitler!" Mrs Sands said, shaking her hand vigorously. Everyone believed the lie that it was Jimmy's. Why wouldn't they? Emily was a married woman who didn't take up with other men. She didn't even look men in the eye. At least once she got a bit fatter, the men who were left behind stopped looking at her. She could thank the demon baby for that at least.

But her bones ached and Emily was seeing eyes everywhere. She could hear the whispers, in her ear, over and over again. It hurt her head. Every day Emily walked to the river and stood at the bank, staring down. The water gurgled and frothed, flowing past. It kept secrets. She wanted to climb in, and let the waters close over her face as she whispered her own secrets, and let it take them away. She wanted to curl up in the cold and let the heat out of her body. She wanted to take her fear and slice it up, make it into weapons, so she could fight the monster man and the man cats. Then Emily could slice up their eyes and the eyes that watched her.

The bombs were coming. They knew for certain, now, that it was a matter of days. The Monster Man had his eyes on them, and he planned to come here. He wanted to fly here and land on their bodies, burnt and broken from the bombs. And he would walk over their necks, plucking his monster babies as he went from still-breathing women, dying on the ground. Emily knew that. He couldn't be stopped. He was as strong as the water, as high as the sky. He was as strong as the demon child that grew in her belly. Emily knew that.

Demon baby moved around a lot now. It was a boy, for certain. He kicked and punched and scratched, from sunrise to sunset. Emily did as much as she could around the house, but it was taking its toll on everyone. Emily wondered if she should go back to her old house, even though it had been boarded up for months. Even though Eddie was closer to Mam than he was to her. There was no talk now of sending them away to the country. Perhaps it was too late for that.

Emily turned away from the river with regret, as the sun lowered itself over the sky. She had to get back in time to pack the children up and head to the shelter. They didn't like it, of course, being packed into a noisy underground railway station with a ton of other people instead of being tucked into their beds, but what else could they do?

They had to do this now, it was wartime. They all had to do their bit. She hated it too, the cold, the noise, the people. It wasn't safe there. There were too many people, and trying to sleep on the floor was just impossible. Emily slept sitting up, back against the wall, hands on both her children. Nonna was miserable too, her face sunken with pain. She wouldn't be surprised if Nonna refused soon, and took her chances with the bombs. Emily would, herself, if it wasn't for Eddie and Betty. They needed her to keep them safe. She would stay with them.

Emily kept a close eye on the setting sun. She never left the house after dark now, not on her own. She hastened her pace, feeling the grind of her joints as she walked. There were three more months to go, if the demon baby arrived on time. As it wasn't human, she didn't know for sure. It could arrive tomorrow for all she knew. She needed a plan, Mam said. Perhaps put the baby up for adoption.

But that wouldn't work. How could she give a demon away? No childless parent would want that. She had to have a better plan. But her mind was empty and tired and broken. She asked in her prayers every night for help but God seemed to have left her alone. Perhaps he was angry about her sin. The Father in Church had said that women had the sin, that women tempted men. Emily was sure he looked right at her when he said it.

She wanted to stand up and shout that she did not tempt the hunting devils but she didn't. Mam had a hand on her waist, keeping her in the seat. Mam's mouth was tight and pinched so maybe Mam saw him look, too. For a godly man, he didn't seem to under-stand much about caring for others.

As Emily neared the house she sent up another quick prayer, just in case God couldn't hear the prayer later from the bomb shelter. *Help me, Father. Help me protect*

my children from the demon that grows inside me. Give me
a sign, and a suggestion of what to do. I'll do the rest. Amen,
Emily.

Emily knew that you weren't supposed to add your
name at the end, but it seemed to her that God got a
lot of requests every day. Adding her name meant that
He would remember that her prayer was hers.

They were waiting for her at the door, the children pale
and scared, her Mam looking tired, her hair tucked
behind her ears. Mam looked cold, despite it being
summer. At least it wouldn't be too cold down in the
shelter. "We were thinking we would have to come and
get you, Emily. You're daydreaming too much."

Her tone was concerned, but cross, like when she was
telling Nonna off for not looking after herself properly.
"Sorry, Mam," Emily said, as she put her hands out
to the children. Betty skipped over, putting her hand
in hers. Her hand was warm and floury, as if she had
just got done baking. Eddie hung back, leaning his
cheek against Mam's leg. Emily left him there. They all
needed whatever comfort they could get right now.

The shelter wasn't far, and there were already people
joining the line, with boxes and coats and blankets in
their arms. People were getting prepared, getting used
to the routine of it. This was a good thing, Nonna said,
because when the bombs started flying, it was hard to
think straight. If your arms knew what to carry, it was
easier. Emily hoped that her arms would know what to
do when the bombs came.

Mam wanted to talk to her about something. Emily
could tell in the fidgety way she moved, and the way her

eyes flicked over to her, back and then over again. She ignored it. She was going to trust that God would give her a sign about what to do, if He wasn't too busy handling the Monster Man over in France, because that was probably more important. Steering planes about was a risky business and He probably had forgotten about handling her small problem.

She still had time. Emily squeezed Betty's hand, twice. Once to remind herself that she was real, and once to tell Betty that she would always be there and not be afraid of the eyes that stared. Betty squeezed back. Their eyes met for just a moment in shared understanding and Emily smiled. She would not be afraid. Tonight, she would not be afraid.

It was still early so there was room to find a spot in the corner and set up. Eddie made minimal fuss about lying on his coat and his blanket, and was mollified by being able to lie next to Mam. Betty took her blanket and wordlessly curled up in what remained of Emily's lap. Nonna strode about on the platform, saying that she may as well stretch her legs before the hordes arrived. Mam just leaned her head against the cool tiled wall, exhausted. Her face looked paper thin.

People were flowing into the shelter, some nodding and saying hello to all and sundry, some floating in as if they were ghosts. Everyone handled the situation differently, Emily noticed. Some really enjoyed the enforced proximity, trying to infuse fun and celebration into the experience. Some just detached, let their souls go, just to survive it.

Emily wondered which one she was. Probably the detached one. She watched the flow, seeing people using the shelter as a way to check in on people, drop extra foodstuffs off, ask favours. It was a night-time hub of sorts, an alehouse without the ale.

Two women stepped over to Mam, wrapped up warmly in shawls and coats and woollen finger-less gloves, despite the season, and handed over small bags of what looked like root vegetables. Mam thanked them genuinely. She wondered if she had seen a tear gleaming at the corner of her eye. These people did not linger, merely handing over their gifts and slipping away. That, Emily decided, was godly. She sent up a thank you prayer for them, just in case God was resting from steering the planes and heard it. These women deserved something back.

A woman drifted in, her coat in one arm and her blanket in the other. Her eyes darted about, looking for a safe place to sit, to sleep. Emily felt the fear of it and caught her eye. *There was space near her. Come take it.* The woman paused for just a moment and then hastened over, pulling her blanket from her arm as if to claim the spot as fast as she could. She sank down, offering quiet thanks.

"I'm Nora. Thank you," she said, her eyes elsewhere as she arranged the blanket over her limbs. The woman was sitting against the wall, her coat tucked under her. It looked like an efficient way to sit, to sleep.

"I'm Emily. You're welcome." Betty was a welcome weight in her lap. It almost made her forget the other weight, burning its way into her skin, growing in her flesh.

Nora's gaze flicked over, seeing her swollen belly. "Oh, congratulations," she said. "You must be thrilled!"

Her tone did not imply that. Perhaps she was tired, but her enthusiasm for a new life coming into the world was absent. Not that Emily minded. She did not have enthusiasm either.

"Thank you," is all she said. Emily did not mind if the woman knew, that this was not a hoped for child. Her two loved babies, they were in this world, now, cuddled by their loved ones. This was not a loved baby. It was not a human baby. Emily knew that. It was a demon baby, one more to swell the ranks of the Monster Man. She was growing the soldier that would kill her own sweet babies. Who would kill her.

Nora assessed her with that swift up and down glance that women always did. It made Emily wonder if she had forgotten to brush her teeth or her hair or something. The inspection, itself, made her come up wanting. Because she never did that, never thought to do that, to others. Emily would never be a real woman.

But Nora did not say anything. She smiled. "Can I come again tomorrow, here? They said we have to keep coming here at night, and I don't want to sleep next to strangers."

Emily nodded. "We'll be here tomorrow. We can save you a space, if you like."

Nora smiled, her relief lighting her smile like stars. "Thank you. Very much." Emily wondered where Nora's family was, why they weren't getting her a space. But she didn't like to ask.

The next day Nora was back, blanket over her hand, walking to the same spot, hopeful. Emily waved her over. Nora subsided with relief. A smile. "You don't know how relieving it is to know where you can put your stuff down. It takes a lot of stress out of this bombing situation."

"Has it started? I know they keep talking about it,"

Nora shot a look, an assessing one. "Not yet. But expect it any day. Keep coming here, like they said to. Claim your spot. It'll be better for your children too, to be in the same place."

She gestured with her head to the demon baby, lodged in her growing belly. "When are you due?"

Emily shrugged. "Three months maybe. In the winter." Her response was flat, toneless, even to her own ear.

Nora watched her with a strange expression, almost a hungry one, as if she had something to offer. But she didn't speak right away, just thinking away behind her eyes.

"And you're not excited?" Nora may have spoken it as a question but she didn't mean it as one. She knew the answer already. Emily didn't need to lie.

"No, I don't want this baby. I tried, you know. It didn't work."

Nora's eyebrows raised a fraction but not by much. It wasn't as if women weren't doing it all the time, what with a war being on, and having little enough to feed the mouths they already had. But people weren't normally open about it.

They just said, oh I must visit with Mrs so-and-so, and raised their eyebrows in a significant way. And the other women would hmm through their noses and nod away. As if it had to stay a secret. Emily didn't understand it, but that was how it was. That was how they did it.

"What will you do then?"

Emily shrugged. "I don't know." Her words were heavy. She didn't know. All Emily knew was that it was too late, that the demon child would have its own way whatever she did. She was just a vessel to carry him until he was big enough to kill them all. She carried her own death. That was the lot of women.

Nora's eyes softened slightly and she pressed her lips together, holding the words in. She patted her awkwardly on the shoulder. "Maybe you'll get an idea. I do know of someone, a place where you can give birth. They handle the after, too."

Emily looked at her, confused. "What do you mean?"

Nora leaned in a bit closer. "They can find a new home for it. You go, you have the baby, and they take it to a new family. You recover and go home back to your life. It's all very simple."

"And how much does it cost? It can't be free. I don't have much money."

"You don't need to worry about that right now. Sometimes she likes to help poor mothers out. She's a good woman."

Emily shivered. If she was a good woman, she would want nothing to do with this baby. But Emily thanked Nora quietly and promised that she would think about it. Mam was lying still with her eyes closed, but Emily suspected she had heard the conversation, even though Nora spoke quietly. That was another Mam trick that she hadn't mastered.

She leaned her head against the wall, trying to tune out the noises around her. It was always loud, even when people were sleeping. It was like trying to sleep in a barn, especially when Mr Miller was there. He sounded like he was driving a tractor with his mouth when he was asleep.

Shutting her eyes, Emily allowed herself to dream for a moment of all the things that could be right in the world. No bombs, no Monster Man. Her Jimmy at home, keeping the cats and eyes away. Just her two children, growing beautifully. And God, listening.

Emily thought of her prayer that she said every day. She did ask for help, and Nora had suggested something. Perhaps it was God, giving her a nudge, so she could help herself. She opened her eyes, thinking to ask Nora how much the woman would want, but Nora was asleep, her dark lashes long against her cheek. She looked peaceful, as if nothing bad would happen to her. She had to have been sent from God. Emily would talk to her Mam tomorrow. And make a plan. She could do this. Shutting her eyes again, she felt lighter. It was three more months. And then she would be free.

GEMMA: CLAIRVOYANTS AND SCREAMS

The clairvoyant arrived with Zoe, looking remarkably normal. She had blonde hair, tied up in a ponytail, and was wearing a black jacket. Gemma felt almost disappointed. There was no bright scarf, no earrings, no jangle of bracelets. She'd definitely been watching too much TV. But the woman seemed friendly and greeted her with a handshake. Zoe introduced her with reverence.

"This is Julie McAffrey, she's the clairvoyant I told you about. I've explained the situation already." Zoe smiled and looked Gemma over. "Are you doing okay?"

"I'm fine. I'm coping." Gemma didn't mention that her heart pounded almost the entire day, and that she could sleep for a week. It was irrelevant right now. Gemma ushered them in, and they removed their jackets. Inside, Ben was already there, waiting with his notebook in front of him. All that lad did was take notes, it seemed. But right now, anything could be useful.

Julie looked around the room with bright eyes. Then she sat, primly, and pulled her bag close to her. "Shall we get started?"

She pulled out an amethyst crystal on a silver chain, and set it beside her. Then she pulled out her own notebook and pen. Gemma started to wonder if she was the only disorganised one in the world, without the urge to write everything down. But she said nothing as she moved closer at Julie's request. Grouped around the small table, the woman lifted the crystal solemnly.

"This is a pendulum, it answers yes and no. A straight line means no and a circle is yes. I'm going to see if I can reach the spirit with it."

The room was dead silent. The woman stared at the pendulum, not speaking. It started to move, slowly, then faster, in a wide circle.

Zoe leaned closer to whisper. "That's freaky, how does it move like that?"

Gemma whispered back. "She could be moving it herself." Zoe sniggered and gave her a small shove.

The pendulum slowed and changed direction, shifting to a side-to-side action, getting faster. Julie frowned, and her lips tightened. Gemma watched her hand closely. To get the pendulum to move that forcefully, the clairvoyant would have to be making it move, but her hand looked still, relaxed. That was weird. At last, the pendulum slowed and stopped.

Julie took a deep breath and looked up. "There is definitely a spiritual presence here, I felt it when I walked in. But the pendulum has confirmed that. I am going to try and contact the spirit and have them speak through me. Sometimes they prefer to use my voice, sometimes they prefer to write, so I give them these options."

Zoe shifted at her side. Gemma wondered if she was going to ask any questions but Zoe remained silent. Ben waited, his pen poised, watching. Gemma noticed that he hadn't written all that much. Perhaps he was waiting for the main event, so to speak.

Gemma turned her eyes back to the clairvoyant who was sitting opposite, eyes closed. She took long, even breaths, hands resting on the table. Then her mouth opened and she started chanting.

"Born of blood, born of blood, born of blood..."

Her voice sounded different, perhaps a little deeper, somehow. Gemma felt a thread of fear wind itself around her throat. Was it getting colder in here, too? Her heart started pounding.

Ben was watching the woman, pen at the paper, but he was pale, and swallowed hard.

From the kitchen there was a rushing sound, as the taps gushed out water. The ghost was here.

Julie winced, and swallowed, and spoke again, this time with her own voice. "We are trying to communicate with the spirit that haunts this place. Is that you?"

The pendulum started to vibrate, and then it lifted into the air. By itself.

Gemma felt her hair standing on end, her face frozen in fear. The silver chain went taut, as if someone invisible were holding it at one end. The pendulum began to move, round and round and round. Yes. That meant yes.

"What is your name?"

The pendulum shifted into a staccato motion, back and forth, in angry movements.

No. No.

Julie's hand jerked, picking up the pen, and then started moving over the paper. Gemma felt the fear in her eyes, holding them open, her gaze fixed on the paper. The pendulum still stayed in the air, impossibly. Shivers racked her body, as the taps sloshed out water, and the pendulum spun in the air, held up by invisible fingers. She was sorry she had ever doubted this woman. But she regretted asking her here. This was horrible. The pen stopped.

On the paper were scratched-out rough letters.

BLOOD. WATER.

Gemma had to ask. "What blood?"

The pen moved again, frantically. The woman, Julie, was blank, her face mannequin-like.

Gemma looked at the word.

YOURS.

Zoe stifled a shriek, covering her mouth with her hand. Gemma wanted to cry, scream, or run, maybe. But she had to ask.

"Are you the water?"

The pendulum spun, round and round.

Yes.

"Am I the blood?" The pendulum kept spinning, faster and faster, catching a gleam from somewhere, glowing. And then, it slowed, swinging to no, and stopped. The pen began to move again, for longer, writing more words.

BORN IN BLOOD. HUNTING. YOU. YOU. YOU. YOU. BLOOD. BLOOD.

Ben was writing frantically, his knuckles white, his face obscured, bent low to the page. Without looking up, he spoke. "What is your name?"

The pen paused for a moment and the taps slowed. It felt like the world had slowed around them. Gemma waited in breathless silence.

At last the pen wrote.

EMILY. I AM COMING FOR YOU. FOR BLOOD.

A scream hung in the air, echoing, resonating. Gemma did not know if it was her or Zoe screaming. Maybe it was both. Zoe was shaking, certainly. And the pendulum stilled, falling onto the table with a screech. The taps stopped. Gemma stared at Ben, who was white as a sheet, with blood on his lip. Perhaps he had bitten it.

The woman slowly returned to herself and fumbled for the pendulum, putting it into her pocket. She looked dazed.

"Did you get what you needed?" Julie asked, as if they had nipped out to the supermarket. Nobody moved.

She looked around at them all, her face considering, and then she got up to leave. "Zoe, just let me know if you want me to come back. I'm happy to do another session, if you're willing."

Zoe heaved herself to her feet, and showed her out. Gemma was glad of that, as her legs felt like water. Ben was looking over his notes, maybe, or just thinking about what to say. Fuck, she didn't even know what to say. A ghost was after her? Why? What would she do? What had she done?

Ben looked up, his eyes serious. "I think someone should stay here at night with you, Gemma. Just in case."

Gemma didn't argue this time.

EMILY: TAKE THE DEMON BABY

The bombs came, just as they predicted. They tore up the ground like they were ravening wolves taking bites out of the roads, out of buildings. Every night the sirens went, and off they went to the shelter, blankets in hand. At first, people sang to drown out the bombs, their eyes wide and glassy with fear.

"Down with Hitler! London will not give up!" and other phrases would bounce around the walls of the tunnels and everyone would cheer.

But now they sat in near silence, listening to the percussion of death raining down over their heads, wondering who would not survive the night. Bad news travelled fast. Some were ghoulish about it, whispering the names of the dead with solemn excitement. Some just listed the names as if they had nipped over the road to buy some tea. "Edna Green died last night, you know. Yeah. Shame. How's your father doing?" It was how they coped.

Emily wanted to howl at the sky, and send the river up into the air, to drown the bombs, and take their teeth away. God was so busy with the planes, he didn't have time to do the bombs, too. She wished she was strong and whole and able to protect everyone.

And when it was dark, and everyone was asleep, Emily indulged in her darkest thoughts. She wished that the bombs would bite and tear the hunting cats, who stalked the streets at night. There were whispers about it now, about women with ripped clothes and tearstained faces, of women who went off with soldiers and got drugged with tainted cigarettes.

The hunting cats were everywhere, riding the bombs, biting the buildings, making women cry.

Emily wished that the war would hurt the right people for a change. But she wished it quietly. She knew it was a wicked thought. She was supposed to forgive, just as God did. But the rage spilled out at night and she could not forgive. Emily wanted to be a hunting cat, but with claws that ripped them in two. She wanted to drown them, and watch them die.

And as the demon baby grew, her darkness grew. She wondered if it would leave when the demon was born, or if it would fill the space it had created in her, if she would walk around with a womb full of bitter rage.

And night after night, the bombs flew.

Her time at last drew nearer. Somehow, Mam had got together the fee for Nora's lady, and Nora had taken it, promising to take Emily to her when the baby was coming.

Nora seemed to know a lot about it, telling her that she didn't have to worry, that Emily could be asleep while the baby came if she wanted, that she wouldn't have to worry about it anymore. Emily nodded and smiled as Nora talked. She didn't think it would be that easy. But that was her secret, and she wasn't telling anyone.

Her small case was packed and waiting in the corner. It was strange to be leaving to have the baby, but it was better. She didn't want the demon to see any of her family's faces, to have a place to come home to. It would be born and see no faces but strangers. It wouldn't know how to follow her home then. Emily would not put her children in danger. Not ever. But she kept her plans secret, only thinking about them when the demon was asleep, when he was not watching her with the eyes that burned.

The day came, with pain and blood, and water rushing from her as if she was the river. Emily was the river, weeping cold tears of pain.

Nora came and bustled her off to the woman, setting her down in a quiet and clean room next to the parlour. There were no other women there, or if they were, they weren't weeping, they weren't screaming. There were no babies.

Emily wondered if they were removed right away, and packed off to empty-handed and empty-bellied women. Her own belly retched, as the demon tried to cleave his way out. His way was blood. She screamed, and screamed again.

A woman arrived, her greying hair tied back in a bun, an apron over her dress. She inspected her quickly in a business-like fashion, putting a hand to her head, to her belly, and then turning back to Nora, nodding just once. She leaned in and stared at Emily.

"Mrs Jones, isn't it?"

Emily frowned, her brow wrinkling. She wasn't called that. She opened her mouth to correct it but she saw Nora shake her head and put her finger to her mouth. Don't say it, she was saying. She looked back at the woman, and realised she did not know the woman's name. Emily was lying in this woman's house, and nobody knew who she was, or where she lived. Would the woman put her in a grave? If it stopped the demon, if it stopped the pain, she would not mind.

The woman was speaking. "Mrs Jones, you are going to have to get undressed and put this gown on. I can give you something to calm you and help you sleep, if you prefer. When you wake up it will all be done, and you can go home. Alright?"

Emily could sleep and then go home. She would not feel the demon climbing out, she would not see its face, it would not see her. "Yes," Emily gasped, riding the wave of blood. She was the river, one keening soul, one wave of tears.

Nora left, and came back with water and a spoon full of a clear liquid. Emily did not stop to look at it, and did not ask what the spoon contained. She took the glass and drank, and then clasped the spoon, putting it between her lips, draining the spoon dry. She threw her head back, panting. She was the river. She was the blood.

Emily's eyes felt glued together. She blinked, and blinked again, letting her heavy eyelids rise and then fall again. There were snatches of light coming in from the nets that covered the window. She was alone, and in bed. Not in her bed, though, she was in the lady's house. Her hands went to her belly, feeling the emptiness, the soft squish of skin, the spongey carcass of where the demon had rested. He was gone. He was gone.

She struggled to rise in the bed, feeling dizzy. Everything hurt. She did not remember it, but her body did. The pain would stay as a reminder. Emily welcomed it. She struggled out of the bed, not sure what time it was, not sure if it was the same day, not sure if she should linger or if she could just go. There was a glass of water on the side, which she drank gratefully. It tasted stale.

Carefully, wincing, she got dressed, took the wrapped linens to stem the bleeding, and left her worn nightdress on the bed. She did not need to stay. Emily looked around the room, and left.

Life was normal again, yet not normal. Emily hugged her children, helped Mam with the chores, and started looking for a job, although Mam said there was no rush for that. Mam hadn't asked about the demon baby, just nodded when Emily returned and said that it was probably for the best. Mam told people quietly that the baby had died, and made sure nobody asked her about it. Emily didn't care anyway. It was gone from her body at last.

But she still heard the baby cry, sometimes, and the milk would begin to tingle, flooding her breasts and making them swell, harden and hurt. It would pass, Emily reminded herself, as she tucked in cabbage leaves and went about her day.

Sometimes she saw a baby scuttling around in ways that it should not move, just out of the corner of her eye. Emily's blood would run cold as she stopped to look again, but there was nothing there.

You saw funny things after having a baby. Emily knew that. It was just her mind playing tricks on her. She stopped up her ears and went about her day, ignoring the corners, ignoring the signs. It was just her imagination. It was fine.

Each night they went to the shelter, but Emily did not see Nora again. She wondered at it. Was she just sent to help her and then she went back to wherever she came from? She wanted to thank her. But at the same time, she was glad. She didn't want the demon to have a link to her, to find her. Emily hoped he was dead, buried somewhere. Even though she knew that was a bad thing to think, even if it wasn't really a baby.

The noises of the shelter calmed her, and even the noise of the bombs. It was normal now, almost like the background ticking of a clock. At first you hated it, and then you got used to it, and then you needed it. That was how it was.

Emily needed that noise, that sitting up against a wall with a toddler in her lap, to even try and sleep. But still, sometimes, as she shut her eyes, she heard him cry. As if he was following her. As if he would never let her go.

Gemma: Seeking the Woman in White

Ben was a reasonable housemate to be around. He left for work early, folding his things up and putting them next to the couch, he washed his dishes and he didn't hog the remote control. He was quite a studious man, doing a lot of work on his laptop in the evenings. But now, he was spending more time researching the Woman in White.

Gemma cooked pasta and Ben leaned against the counter at the end, eyes on the screen. Having him there helped with her nerves, that was for sure: it didn't stop the nightly visits but she wasn't jumping at shadows anymore. He adjusted his position, wincing as he stretched his back, and reached for his coffee. He took it with milk and two sugars. NATO standard, he called it. He always made her a coffee for when she got in from work which was thoughtful, but he left her to decompress. He didn't bother her with questions. In a different circumstance, they would get on much better, probably.

"I think I may have found something on the name of the ghost," Ben said, putting the mug to his lips. He didn't look over.

"You've found the ghost's name, you mean?"

Ben shook his head. "No, not the name in particular. But I was looking up the name Woman in White, as it rang a faint bell. There's a Hungarian myth about a Woman in White, but there are a lot of myths in this country about a White Lady. She's typically in a white dress, and is associated with a place of tragedy." He stopped reading and raised his eyebrow meaningfully. "Now I don't know about you, but I wouldn't think the former prison was a holiday camp."

Quite. Gemma wondered, not for the first, and not for the last time, if she had been blatantly stupid to bid for a house on the site of a former prison. She would never do that again, once this was over. If it ever was, over.

"What happened to them?"

"The women? Well, the myths vary, but they all seem to have met sad ends. Some died or killed themselves after losing children. That's horrible."

Ben had noticed something, if his intent expression was anything to go by.

Gemma shivered as the water began to boil and turned the heat down. She might have to resort to oven-baked food for the interim. Anything to avoid the sound of water bubbling.

It took a moment before Ben surfaced again, his face thoughtful. "There aren't many instances of a White Lady being associated with water, though. Perhaps it's where our ghost died. She might have drowned. Emily."

Gemma winced. "Don't say her name like that. I don't want to think of it as a person. Please."

Ben nodded. "Good point." Silence fell, punctuated by the odd tap of keys.

Gemma prepared food, trying to avoid the sink as much as she could. It wasn't like the ghost had accosted her at the sink, not yet, but it could switch the taps on at will so she was wary of them.

She had never gone through so much dry shampoo in her life. Gone were the long, leisurely baths or hot showers. She showered at Zoe's house, usually, but she was in and out as fast as she could, just in case. She didn't want to draw the ghost into Zoe's house. She had enough going on right now.

"How is Zoe?"

It was as if Ben could read her mind. "She's doing okay, I think. She's not coming tomorrow with Wes, but she said she's fine. She just has to rest a bit. And Wes doesn't want her to stay here and get frightened, obviously."

Ben just nodded. "Complicated things, pregnancy." His face looked nervous, uncomfortable, perhaps. It was clearly not in his area of expertise. Nor hers, really, either, even though she had studied nursing. She had focused from the start on mental health, knowing that was where she wanted to go. Rosy-cheeked infants and women in labour were not in her career path. But now she wished she knew a bit more, so she could reassure Zo as she went on this journey without her. She just wanted to keep her safe. Somehow.

EMILY: SAVING THE CHILDREN

I t was spring. The rains were washing the streets clean, or what was left of them, and the sun was beginning to get stronger. Mam and Nonna had spring colds. Eddie was getting big, and talkative, and wanted to go out and play with the boys in the street. Betty was still her baby, even though she was walking confidently and getting into everything. Her Jimmy had even written a very short letter to say that he was alright and missed them. Emily should have been happy.

Emily had to be happy. She smiled when Mam or the babies looked at her, but she couldn't get it to reach her eyes. Nonna watched her, all the time.

Emily wondered if Nonna saw the demon baby too. It cried a lot, still, at night. Sometimes she heard the skitter of feet as a creature skidded past, sliding into a corner. She should be happy, but she could not be, because she was afraid.

He had found her. It was too long after the birth now, it couldn't be that. It was him. He was back. And he was going to hurt the babies. He was going to claw them, and leap on them, and rip them in two. Emily had to do something. She had to save them. Emily had to be the hunter cat now.

As she walked to the river, she called up to the sky, just in case God had any help for her. But there was nothing but the grey clouds and a dull sky. Perhaps she was out of chances. Mam had tried to help, and God sent Nora, but the demon child was going to do what he was going to do anyway. This time Emily would be ready. She knelt at the water's edge and put her hands in, feeling the water gently lap at her hands. The water was the key. It would save them. Emily leaned closer and whispered to the water. "I know you'll help me. You've always helped me."

She felt the pain and worry ease out of her hands, cooling her arms and making her head feel clear. Out here, there were no demon cries. There were no scuttling sounds of deformed limbs, or the hiss of a whisper. She did not feel his shadow preparing to jump onto her back, claws bared. He had not found her here. Not yet. But he would, soon. Soon, he would follow her out of the house, and he would swallow up the water, swallow up the world. Emily knew this.

Reluctantly, Emily straightened, feeling the ache in her hips and her back still. She had not recovered quickly from this pregnancy, it had taken its toll on her, leaving strands of grey in her hair, and creaks in her joints. She felt as if she had been given a decade of years to carry on her tired back. She waved a tiny farewell to the river as she turned back to the house, trudging back up to the road. She wouldn't stay away long this time. The river would wait.

Nonna was sleeping and Mam was heading out some-where, to run some errands and stop in on a widow a few streets away. Emily smiled genuinely for the first time in months, and Mam nearly cried. Touching Emi-ly's face gently, Mam smiled too, and promised to come back with something nice for tea. Emily treasured the moment.

Gathering the children, she bundled them into their coats and boots, as they were going to see the river. She packed a small basket with a sandwich and a flask of warm drink, which the children eyed greedily. Emily promised that they would have a proper picnic as soon as they got there. Sending them outside quietly, she shut the door as carefully as she could.

So as not to wake Nonna, she reasoned, but Emily knew it was to make sure the demon didn't hear and follow them. She didn't have much time.

The sun was descending over the sky, but not yet near setting. They settled at the bank and enjoyed their picnic, the children's high voices dancing in the air. It was nice for them to be outside, to not have to worry about the bombs, to not have to be afraid. Emily tou-sled Eddie's hair, and stroked Betty's face. They were beautiful and perfect and good.

It was not long before the sedative in the drink took effect, and their eyes closed, their little bodies stilling in a deep slumber, side by side on the bank.

Emily did not know how much was right for children, but it did not matter. She needed them to be asleep for the river to take them. More was better than less. There was probably enough in that drink to send a horse to dreamland. Emily eyed the flask longingly. There probably wasn't enough for her, and she had to be alert to fight the demon baby if he came. There wasn't much time.

Eddie was much heavier as a dead weight than she expected, and Emily hesitated. She needed to send them together. They could not be alone. She was sure about that.

Staggering, she adjusted Eddie onto her right hip, and then leaned for Betty. Her dark lashes were so long, so perfect, against her beautiful face. She would become such a beautiful young woman. Emily steeled herself. She had to protect them. Her little Betty could never be mauled by the cats. Or touched by the demons. No.

Emily took a breath and hauled her up, letting Betty's head loll against her neck.

Just for a moment Emily breathed in the scent of her daughter, and then her son. She placed a kiss on Eddie's forehead, and turned, walking into the river. The water curled around her legs, slowing her motion, but helping her support her children, her babies, as she got nearer. The ground of the river descended steadily, slowly, until it was deep enough. She stood in the water with them cuddled against her, as she watched the sun come out from the clouds and speckle the river with golden light. It was time. This was God's hour.

Emily looked up to the sky. "I'm sending them to you, God. You need to look after them now. Betty doesn't like peas, and she gets frightened sometimes at night. Eddie is a strong boy, and he'll look after his sister.

You need to look after them until the demon baby goes away. I know they'll be safe with you."

Tears burned in her eyes. "Please tell them I love them, God," Emily whispered, as she let them slowly drop into the water and disappear from sight.

GEMMA: A GUARD'S TALE

They pulled up in an overgrown estate in North London somewhere, with crowded houses and dirty windows. All it needed was a few abandoned cars and a sofa in a garden to make it a stereotype of its own. Wes led the way, knocking on one of the doors and turning back to her with a tired smile. "He will believe you. Don't worry."

Gemma almost smiled. She was a long way from worrying if someone would believe her. She was more worried that she wouldn't live through this horror without losing her mind.

Her hand went back to her wrist, or more accurately, the gap on her wrist where her bracelet should be. That was from her dad, and she could have sworn she left it on her bedside cabinet. But it wasn't there when Gemma woke up, and the absence of it was bothering her.

The door opened to a plain hallway with grey-carpeted stairs in the background. The man looked old, his face lined. But his eyes were sharp, and he took them both in before smiling at Wes. "Nice to see you, Wes. Thanks for coming. Come in!"

He turned, walking back into the house, as they followed. Gemma locked the door carefully behind her. It probably wouldn't keep the ghost out but she did it anyway, just in case.

"Do you want coffee?" The voice floated back. Wes answered, remembering how she drank her coffee, too. She would have to text Zoe later and award him man points for that.

She thought of Ben, who also got it right, and grudgingly awarded him some, too. He was of course a good man. But she would have preferred to not be in the situation of needing a bodyguard who knew how she took her caffeine.

The sitting-room was full of clocks. Gemma started to count them, and gave up when she got to twenty. That was just crazy. It looked as if someone had pulled off a grand heist in Switzerland and brought all the clocks back. She wondered if he had a wife, or if it was his not so secret passion.

Gingerly, she sat down on a chair, hoping it didn't belong to the owner of the chair. She needed his help, not his ire.

The man bustled back in, offering her a chipped mug with a faded image of the Queen on it. She thanked him, putting it on the floor in front of her. Wes and the man exchanged a few moments of pleasantries, as Gemma listened. She knew they worked together, but it was clear that Wes had respected the man. His face lit up and he leaned forward as if he was in front of his favourite teacher at school. That was nice. The man seemed to enjoy it too, coming back to one of his mentees. She wished she could remember the man's name. Wes had mentioned it, but she couldn't keep a thing in her head lately. Burns, maybe. Something like that.

The man turned to her, offering his hand to shake. His hands were old but his handshake was not; his grip was strong and solid. He looked at her with clear, blue eyes. "I'm Barnes. Wes knows me as Barnes, or Officer Barnes, but you can call me Barnes, or David if you prefer. And Wes tells me your name is Gemma?"

"Yes, Officer, er, David. I'm Gemma."

Barnes smiled. "And you work for the hospital, is that right?" The man released her hand at last, keeping it for just a little too long. Gemma resisted the urge to wipe her hand clean. While she sympathised with the loneliness that older people felt, she did not want to become their support human. Especially not now, when she had her own problems.

"That's right. St Pancreas."

Barnes took the point, smiling again but returning to business, leaning back in his chair and looking at Gemma, then Wes. "And what can I do for you today? I don't think for a moment that you came all the way out here to talk about the weather!"

Wes sat forward, clasping his hands loosely on his legs. "We've come to talk to you about the Woman in White, Barnes."

The atmosphere changed. Barnes sat up slightly, his attention sharpening. "What do you want to know?"

"Well, I know you saw her a few times in Holloway, you warned me about her yourself. But I wondered if you knew about her origins, who she visited, and how ... dangerous she is."

Barnes frowned. "Dangerous? I don't know about that, lad, she was scary as hell, I won't deny, but I never got a dangerous vibe from her personally. Mind, I should say that I saw her, but she never came to see me specifically. But I heard about her a lot. Hmmm."

Barnes stroked his beard and moustache for a moment, deep in thought. "I started my probation at Holloway, you know, and then I went up north for a while before I came back. So I've not seen all that much of our White Lady. I've seen a fair few other ghosts, I must say, in my time. But they warned me about her when I arrived. I didn't believe it, of course. I knew better and I thought they were a bunch of superstitious housewives." He laughed, and Wes laughed. Barnes nodded to Gemma in apology. "I mean no offence, lass, it's just the way I speak."

Gemma nodded. It was irrelevant if he did mean offence or not. And they needed to find out more about the ghost anyway.

"But I saw her and I had to eat my words. She turned up one night when I was on patrol, and nearly scared the wits out of me. I was doing a night check, you know, check the cells, make sure everyone is alive, and there she was, walking along in front of me, bold as brass.

She was wearing a long white dress, and her hair was unbound. And every step left a patch of wet, a little puddle. As if she were made of water. She just walked in front like she was Florence Nightingale, doing her own check. I didn't see her much after that, which I am glad of, I'll be frank. That first night I ended up paralytic in the local bar as I couldn't stop shaking. Everyone laughed at me, of course."

This didn't make any sense. "So she wasn't scary? She didn't hunt anybody?"

Barnes turned to Gemma, assessing her. "Oh, she was certainly scary. I've never been so frightened in my whole life. But I got off lucky, for some reason. She never hunted me. She did hunt some others, though. There were a few in my time that got a lot of visiting from the Woman in White. Yup."

"And what happened to them?" The words flew out of her mouth, unbidden. His eyes narrowed slightly, and Gemma saw shadows of the man he was underneath, the one who kept prisoners at bay, the one with the power.

"The officers? Some met a sticky end. It wasn't always at the prison, but it was, sometimes. Some said that she was trying to drown them, that she was hunting them. Some transferred to other prisons, and I didn't see them again. Some died at home. But it wasn't always. Either she liked you, or she didn't. And I wouldn't want to be one of the people she didn't like!"

Barnes laughed, hard, clutching his chest. Wes and Gemma didn't join him.

Subsiding, he looked again at both of them. "Something tells me you're not doing a history report on the prison. What's going on?"

Wes spoke up first, glancing at Gemma. "Well, Gemma here moved into the apartments that are built on the grounds of the prison. And now she's being haunted by the Woman in White."

Barnes started, nearly dropping his coffee. "She's doing what? In your house?"

"Yes. She's rising up through the floor every night, and she turns the taps on, flooding my place. We got a clairvoyant in and she wrote on the paper, she said she was hunting me, that she was coming for me." Her voice shook. It always shook when she admitted it. That Gemma was on a ghost hit-list.

Barnes shook his head, his eyes filled with worry. "That's not good at all, and not what I was expecting to hear. I don't remember her ever being a danger to the prisoners. I always got the impression she was there to watch over them. Clearly, I was wrong."

He sat back in his chair, pursing his lips. "What do you need from me, Wes? Gemma? Is there any way I can help?"

"Unless you know a way of stopping a dangerous ghost from killing me, I don't think you can help, David. But thanks. Do we need anything else, Wes?" Gemma was done, rising from the chair. Wes started to stand, then paused. "Thanks, Barnes. Can you get the details on the officers who were attacked by the ghost?"

Barnes got to his feet. "Of course. I'll send it to you. Or to you, Gemma? I wonder if there is a way to stop her, though. I've always thought that the Woman in White was a person who died in the prison. Now there weren't that many prisoners that died there, unless they were executed. It wouldn't be difficult to check public records for the hangings. If you can find a name, you might be able to reason with her, perhaps. It's a long shot, but I guess right now you're out of options."

"It's a good idea. Thanks, David." Gemma reached out and shook his hand again. This time he took her hand in both of his and looked closely into her eyes. "I hope you'll be okay, Gemma. I really do. I'm sorry this happened. Prisons can cause a lot of misery, it sticks around. Even when the prison itself is taken away. If I find anything I'll call you right away. And, stay safe."

Tears pricked her eyes. If only she could stay safe. She nodded, removing her hand, and headed for the door, letting Wes handle the farewells. She barely reached the door of his car before she started to cry.

EMILY: A NOOSE AND A CURSE

Quietly, Emily turned the handle and walked back into the house as the sun subsided behind her. The house was in darkness. It took her a moment to see Nonna in the chair, waiting. Her face was lined, her eyes streaked with grief. Nonna shook her head. "Emily. What have you done?"

Her voice was pained. Emily opened her mouth to reassure her, that it was alright, that they were safe, but Nonna waved her hand to stop her speaking and put it to her mouth, her face working, tears spilling from her face. Strange sounds came from her mouth, almost laughing, but they were ripped from her chest, raw and loud. Nonna must be grieving.

Emily watched, wondering at it. Who did she grieve? Surely Nonna understood? Surely, Nonna, of all of them, understood? She knew about the devils.

"I had to keep them safe, Nonna."

Her words were clear and calm.

Nonna nodded, crying so hard it was as if the river was spilling from her eyes. She said something but it was so quiet, hidden behind the sobs, that Emily did not hear it. She leaned closer, wishing that she could be as small as Betty and climb onto Nonna's lap.

At last, she heard it. "I know, child. I know."

The trial was loud. Every day they roused Emily with loud voices and sent her to the wooden room where the man stared at her with his stone-chip eyes, listening to what people said. He never asked her about the hunting cats, or the demon baby.

He just kept staring at her, his hand holding up his head, as people talked in ways that she could not follow.

Emily stood there, as she was told to, in the wooden room, but she did not understand why. Why were they not fighting the monster man? Why were they not hunting the Cats who were hurting the women? It didn't make any sense.

They were all made to stand and say something in the box in front of the hard faces. Her family had to stand, who couldn't look at her, except for Nonna and Mam, who did, but their eyes were wet, their faces drawn. They answered the questions, trembling, and sank back to their seats. Emily didn't understand. Why were they talking about her, and not the cats who hunted?

The next day a familiar face was made to stand, wearing clothes much like Emily did. Nora was at the stand, and she did not look over, not once, yet the judge was not friendly and soft to her like he was with Mam and Nonna. Emily watched, confused.

The judge asked if Nora had taken money for a service from the defendant. Emily thought that might be her. She wanted to answer but they waved her silent. That didn't make much sense. She could explain this quickly enough. But they didn't want her to speak.

Nora spoke to hard eyes who did not want to listen to her, either. Emily leaned forward, afraid. She did not know what she was afraid of, but she knew that she was. Why were they wasting time asking women strange questions? Why weren't they asking the real questions? It didn't make sense.

They grew tired of Nora's answers and they dragged her away, roughly. Emily hoped that Nora would be alright. She had looked after her and she should not be treated badly. But the judge still looked stern and would not look at her. He did not even ask her anything about what Nora said.

At last, he did some writing in his big book and then reached down, fumbling for something.

He came back up with a black square of cloth which he placed carefully on his head. There was an eruption of murmuring, and some started to cry. Emily watched, fascinated.

The judge started speaking, in words that she did not understand. She heard death, and murder, but then Emily got lost.

At last he looked at her with his cold, dead eyes. "May God have mercy on your soul," he said.

And arms took her fast and dragged her back down the stairs, and Emily was afraid.

It was a corridor of doors in the prison. Each door had a face at it, looming, and each door echoed with rage. It was as if they were trying to break out of their cells, banging on them, over and over, as Emily walked past. Dragged was probably more accurate. Her legs didn't work, she was frozen with fear.

She was in the dark and the faces stared, and leered, and grinned, and snarled. And the noise carried on, breaking into her brain, hurting her ears.

Emily understood it, now, at last. She hadn't understood in the big room but listening to the guards speaking about her had helped. They thought she had murdered her children. And of course they would be angry! She would be angry too, if someone had murdered her child.

Emily had saved hers. But she had not been given the chance to explain that.

She knew they wanted to kill her. She knew that the judge was going to kill her. She was alone in the dark, waiting to die. Emily sent a prayer up to God.

Hello, God. Please don't forget to check on Betty as she gets frightened. If you can tell her I'll be there soon, I'd be grateful. Eddie would love to play with more friends, if you could give him that. Thank you, Emily. She added the Emily just in case he got confused, hoping that her babies would know her name was Emily and confirm it was her.

At least they went up together. That had to be a blessing.

She heard a creak and a hole opened, showing part of a face with hard eyes looking at her. She wondered if it was a guard.

It just stared at her for a moment, cold eyes gleaming, and then she saw the mouth.

"They'll kill you soon, I reckon. Do you want to know how they'll do it? They'll hang you. Right here in Holloway. They'll cover your face up so nobody sees you turning black, and then they'll dump your body in the grounds. Your family won't want your corpse back, not after what you've done. Child Killer. You're going to hell."

"I didn't kill them. I saved them."

The hole was closing but it opened again, the eyes flashing back, spitting hate. "Is that your excuse, devil?

You killed those poor wee mites. And your baby. She's dying too, you know. Your friend. She'll probably die next to you. If you ask nicely, perhaps they'll let you watch. She can hold the door of Hell open for you. Evil witch. Murderer."

Emily shook her head. He was wrong. Fear seeped in. What did he mean by her friend? "Who? Who is my friend?"

The guard paused, looking at her with a sneer on his face. "Wheatly. The one who told the court what you did to make sure you'd hang. You'd hang anyway for the other two babies but three, that's even worse. She thought she'd get off with it, see. But she's hanging, too, just like the other one. They're baby farmers. The devils were taking money from decent God fearing women and killing the babies. Eating them too, most probably. You're all as bad." His mouth came close to the hole and spat. "Satan's whores!"

The hole slammed closed and left her in the dark. Emily's mind whirled. She had never heard of baby farmers before. But it was calling them devils that made her pause. Were they devils too? Had she done the wrong thing? The demon was still out there, growing. And she was locked in here. She dug her fingers into the ground, shaking. Was she going to Hell? What if God didn't take her children into safe-keeping?

Tears ran down her face and she screamed, again, and again.

Her soul cleaved in two, in grief, in agony.

As she screamed she heard women's voices laughing, cheering, shouting "Murderer! Devil! You die soon! Hell's waiting for you, whore!"

Emily screamed again, letting her rage flow, and the darkness that swirled in her body swept out of her mouth. She screamed and she cursed. She cursed the prison, she cursed the women, and she cursed herself. Again and again and again.

By the time they came for her she was spent.

She did not react or beg as they bundled her off, one guard on either side, holding her as if she would escape. Why would she? This was the end of her journey. Her blood stopped here.

Emily stared forward without seeing anything. All she could think of was Betty's soft hair, her eyelashes that curved against her cheek. Of Eddie's smile as he drank his last drink.

She imagined them holding hands standing on clouds, up high, with Jesus reaching out to them.

A light touched her face from the one window in the room. She looked up at it. *Thank you, God,* she prayed. *Even if I'm off to the bad place for what I did, I know you've got them. I'm going to keep the demons far away from them. I'm going to be the river guardian.*

Emily did not listen to the words spoken by the witnesses, stuffed into suits and stern faces. She did not blink when they covered her face in linen and put the rope around her neck, tying her hands behind her back. She just looked up to where the light was, and smiled. She would stay here, and chase the devils. She would

make them scream, and drown, and die. She would
make them all die.

GEMMA: CONFRONTING THE PAST

The building of the British Library loomed above her. It was huge. She knew it was big, but she had never really appreciated the sheer scale of it. It took her breath away, with its red brick gleaming in the sun and the imposing turrets. Gemma was glad to be alone.

There had been enough disagreeing that wasn't quite arguing before she was 'allowed' to go by herself to the library, even though it was the same stop that she used for work, so hardly out of her way, and what was going to happen anyway? Gemma wasn't going mad, she was being haunted. Why was she being treated as if she were ill?

Her hands shook as she searched through her bag for the paper that she needed. Ben had written it all down in his careful script of what to ask for. And she was forgetting things again. Just this morning she had found her watch in the fridge, and her perfume wasn't in its usual place.

She couldn't even remember what she watched last night on TV. But that was the trauma, too. Anyone would struggle with being haunted. Anyone.

It was cool inside the library, and it was quiet. No dripping of taps, no pools of water. If only she could sleep there without the risk of the books getting waterlogged. The reception staff were helpful, directing her to the archives, and it was a nice walk.

Gemma was thankful again that she had not just done this at home on Ben's laptop. She wanted to do something alone for a change. She was not cut out to have someone around her all the damn time. It was strange to be around people, though. She clutched her bag, wishing she had found her dad's bracelet. She had searched everywhere. At this rate she was going to confront the ghost and demand that it give her shit back. The haunting was one thing but taking her stuff was beyond the pale.

A small voice in her head reminded her that things were disappearing long before the ghost turned up, but she suppressed it. She hadn't lost the bracelet. No way.

Gemma followed the signs for the Archives, and turned into a large room lined with computers and files. She paused for a moment, a little overwhelmed. Would she need to load the film into the machines, or leaf through thousands of old newspapers?

She approached a member of staff, asking for advice quietly. The man directed her to the computers, adding helpfully that all of the archives for newspapers were available online, anyway. Great. So she could have stayed at home. Well, she was here, and she would take advantage of the quiet.

Tapping at the keys, she started with searching for deaths in prison. That brought up hundreds of thousands of results. Scrolling through, she caught sight of details of crimes, accidental deaths, and illness. She considered what to do for a moment, then amended the search to death in Holloway prison.

She may as well start there. As she hadn't moved from the old site, it stood to reason that she had died there. That seemed to do the trick, returning only 40,000 hits. Her eyes found a first case, a woman who died of illness but the prison staff thought she was drunk. Clearly, the healthcare in 1929 was as good as it was nowadays.

Gemma paused over one tiny article about a baby who had died in prison. She didn't know there were babies in prison, too. But then, if both parents were in prison, where would the baby go? She wiped a tear as she moved on. There was so much death. More children, or local children that had died, men and women who had died by accident, or of illness, or by their own hand. She noticed an article that mentioned a man who had died in prison after being released from a Japanese prison camp. But this wasn't her ghost. Regretfully, she moved on.

The words "death cell" caught her eye. That sounded rather forbidding. Quickly, she went back up to the search and put in 'death cell, Holloway' and started to read the entries. There was woman after woman, sentenced to die, waiting in a cell separately, one that they would come out of only once.

She went back up again, hesitated, then added, 'Emily' to the search.

The computer whirred.

It took only a few articles before she spotted an Emily, who had been charged in 1940 with a triple murder of her children. Her hands began to shake as she opened the article, zooming in a little so she could read the scanned page. The headline was dramatic of course, calling her a Child Murderess. Gemma read on. The woman had killed her three children in cold blood, it said, drowning her two older children of 4 and 2, and being involved in a plot to kill a newborn baby.

She made a note of the other names, a Wheatly and a Cole, who were co-conspirators. She would look them up. The convicted woman drowned her children. It had to be her. Quickly, she picked up her phone, sending a quick text to Ben and Wes.

> Gemma: I found her. There was an Emily who was hanged in Holloway for killing her three children. She drowned two of them.

She checked the surname and did a search for that particular prisoner, noting absently that it had made not only the local but the national newspapers. It must have been a big thing at the time. The country was at war by then, weren't they? Gemma cursed her gaps in history. It was never her subject.

Her phone pinged, and pinged again. Ben replied asking for details, a name, or something, so he could do some more research, and Wes just replied with, "Got her!" And a thumbs up. She sent a quick message back to Wes.

> Gemma: Best keep Zo out of this. I don't want the ghost knowing about, you know.

> Wes: Will do. X

Gemma smiled, just slightly. Yes, she wouldn't get to see her best friend for what could be the foreseeable, but if this creature was a child-killer, then she wasn't allowing a pregnant woman near Zoe. It was as simple as that.

She did another search, this time for Emily, and her original address, and her crime. If the ghost was going to hunt? Then so was she. So was she.

Gemma and Ben compared notes together, spread out over the floor, with a pizza and a bottle of wine. Gemma was surprised that Ben got her usual one: he was clearly observant. Not that she cared really what type of wine she drank, but he picked up the one she usually bought. It must be a popular brand, maybe. She tended to just look for white and look for the one on offer, but that one usually was selling cheap. Perhaps nobody else wanted to drink it. But today she was glad of it, and even felt sad that there wasn't another bottle. She almost felt human today, and she hadn't felt like that in a while.

Ben was animated, when his head wasn't in his computer, doing various searches and general research on the woman, the area, and the case. As Gemma had seen, it had hit the national headlines, and for good reason. The city hadn't seen a baby farmer in almost forty years.

"So, what did they do, exactly? Take the babies and kill them? Were they trafficking the women, too? Supplying rich families with babies?"

"I'm not sure. It appears to be that they took unwanted babies and promised that they would go to rich families, and then killed them off."

"But they were unwanted. I'm not promoting killing babies, not in the least. But if there wasn't abortion, what else could women do?"

Ben shrugged. "I don't know. I think the poor women were paying these farmers to take the babies, maybe in good faith. Everyone seems to hate the baby farmers though. I hope they weren't cruel to the babies."

That did not bear thinking about. Gemma shuddered. "And this... ghost... she was one of these baby farmers?"

She took another mouthful of her wine, wondering if she should just risk it and run to the shop. More wine was far too tempting. Not feeling. Just floating. She put the glass down. It would probably go down even faster if she kept hold of it.

Ben frowned, his attention on the laptop. He had hardly touched the drink, or the pizza. He wasn't a big junk food fan, then.

"It's hard to tell from these articles. She doesn't look involved more than paying for the service, and she might have not known what they were going to do. But one reporter said that she did not speak, nor showed a scrap of remorse. Not even when they sentenced her to death."

"That's weird. Wouldn't she be at least upset if they were killing her? How did they kill her? Was it in the prison?"

"One second," Ben said, clicking away on the keys. "They hanged her. Yes, in the prison. So on the premises, so to speak. Ugh, that's spooky."

"It's probably why she haunts the place. She wants to hurt everyone." Gemma drained the glass, and Ben eyed it for a moment. "Here, have mine. I don't drink much."

She wouldn't turn that down. She took it, gladly. Perhaps she would sleep better tonight.

As the night cooled and the moon retreated, she woke, as she always did. Gemma's room was bright, bathed in cold light, and the dark water poured in. Even as her breath caught and her heart pounded, something deep in her traumatic brain delighted in it, in the consistency of it. Fear, she understood. At least it made sense, unlike the days, when nothing did, anymore. Gemma might be terrified, but at least there was an honesty about it.

Even as her heart screamed and clutched at her throat, there was a calmness about her tonight. Gemma watched with a detachedness, a separateness from her own body. This was her reality. The ghost came, and tormented, and then she left. The ghost's head emerged, splitting the black water that lapped at her quilt, that she did not dare touch, or move away. She kept her hands firmly inside the bed, away from the water.

And then it floated forward, face, staring, with dark black eyes, dripping hair, white dress.

Gemma's face was frozen. But her mouth managed to spit out one word. "Emily."

It was the first time. The first time Gemma had spoken, the first time she had named her. She did not know why that word had fallen from her mouth, did not know why the ghost stilled, and drew back. But then, it looked, and locked eyes with her. Gemma could not look away. All she could see was the blackness of her eyes. Just her eyes.

She fell into a dream.

Gemma flowed behind the ghost, watching a life that did not look like her own, a London that did not look like her own. She flew past a child growing, laughing, of a young light-haired woman marrying a handsome young man, of moving into a new home. And then it slowed, and the clouds gathered over the river that rushed by. It was a huge river, tinted with gold. Gemma looked out at it, wondering where it was. It was beautiful.

Smoke grew and clung to the buildings. People drew themselves close, clutching jackets and hats, scurrying past. They were afraid. And then she saw a young woman, looking right at her on the other side of the road. Her face was serious, sad.

Emily. It had to be her. By mentioning her name, she had come. Emily started to walk, heading away from her, so Gemma followed.

Laughter filled her ears, and then two children danced past: one boy, his knees grazed, with a wide smile. He was so blonde that his hair almost caught fire in the light. He laughed and laughed, his eyes sparkling. A small girl chased him, still a little unsteady on her feet, with her hair tied in a plait. She was calling for him. Sometimes he would turn back and look, and laugh, and run on again.

Gemma cast her eyes to the ghost. She still did not look, but her eyes were fixed on the children, her hand reaching out ever so slightly. It was almost as if she mourned them. But how could she, she had killed them, that made no sense!

There was a third child. She looked around for the third child, one that had to still be a proper baby, not walking about. Gemma saw none.

The ghost walked on, so Gemma followed. The clouds drew darker, swooping low, driving past in strange directions, as if the clouds were shooting to the earth. She turned into a quiet road, that began wide, and got more narrow, with a river on one side. Gemma struggled to keep up, hurrying as best she could, and then she saw shapes detaching themselves from the wall, walking towards the woman in front. The ghost was oblivious.

"Wait!" Gemma tried to call. "Stop! Look!" Her words did not come out, just faint wisps of air that rose up to form with the clouds that clustered closer, the audience, the show. She felt her heart pounding again, but not from fear. Gemma knew this story, and she knew that it would not end well.

"Stop!" she shouted again, but the shapes drew nearer, surrounding the woman, and then the smoke dissolved them all, their silhouettes dispersing and flowing away on the breeze. The hunched clouds regarded her for a moment before retreating, leaving her with a perfect rose-gold sky. Gemma realised she was crying, hot, wet tears, flowing fast.

She knew. She knew what had happened.

GEMMA: I DON'T THINK SHE'S A MONSTER

"I'm not saying you're right or wrong, Gemma. I'm just concerned, here. You've had a dream about the ghost, and now you think she's not dangerous. We were all there when she said she was going to hunt you, and she comes to you every night. I see the water under the door, every night. Men have died in the prison when she hunted them. I'm just wondering if it's getting too much. Maybe you should, I don't know, see someone professional about it. Get some therapy."

Gemma pushed her frustration back down. Ben was a friend, and she was grateful to him, but she did not welcome him suggesting she needed psychiatric help. "Yes, I had a dream, and I think it's worth following up. What if it's true, that she was attacked? I bet that happened all the time in those days. Lots of people go mad when they have to carry a rape baby. I think she's trying to tell her story. Didn't you say it was worth trying to contact her? But now I have, you're telling me I'm wrong."

Ben huffed, pushing his glasses back up on his nose. "I just think you're taking unnecessary risks, Gemma. You're already not sleeping well, you're not eating much, and, well, you know. I just think you need to consider another option."

"Like what?"

He paused. "Moving out, maybe. Get somewhere else. I know you've not long moved here, but it's clearly not good for your health. What about going back to your dad's place?"

Gemma paused. "How did you know I used to stay with my dad?"

He didn't appear to hear the question, looking into his phone in a studious fashion. At last, he shrugged. "Not sure. Maybe Wes told me."

Gemma thought it over. Wes did talk a lot, and she was probably being paranoid. She let it lie. "I'm not moving, anyway. I just got this place, and Emily can simply move on. She's in the past."

"I thought you didn't want to call her that?"

"Well, it feels different now. I saw her as who she used to be. If she was raped, I can understand how bad that must be."

Ben was staring at her, his eyes intent, fixed on her face. "You aren't like that woman. She was a bad person. You're special."

Gemma shifted, uncomfortably. "I'm not special. I'm quite ordinary. Anyway, I'm going to ask Zo to contact that clairvoyant, and get her to come back. And if that works, then I think she's not going to be dangerous, after telling her story. You'll be able to move back to your own place. I'm sure you're dying to get your own space back!"

I know I am, she thought. But Gemma didn't want to offend him. He nodded and murmured something, before gathering up some things and disappearing for a shower. She shrugged. It wasn't as if he was going to live there forever. It was good to remind him of that before he got his feet under the table. It's not even like they were a 'thing'.

A niggling doubt crawled into her head, lodging itself uncomfortably in her chest. He didn't think they were a thing, did he? Why did he say special like that?

She shook the thought away. She was overthinking, as usual. It was probably nothing.

Zoe came back quickly, eager to help. She said that the medium would visit again, this time with Wes, as Zoe was still banned from coming, just in case. Gemma wondered if she should mention the dream, but didn't want to upset her friend. She was pregnant and that could do funny things to your mood. No, she wouldn't say anything. But she would speak to Wes. He would understand.

Flipping through her old university books, she looked up ante-natal and post-natal depression. She had studied it at the time, but hadn't encountered it since starting work in a geriatric psychiatric ward. It wasn't likely that her patients would be upping and getting pregnant. The words swam before her eyes. Depression, hallucinations, depersonalisation, mood swings. It was all very vague.

She needed more than that. Feeling a spark of her old energy, she gathered her things, leaving a note for the housemate who was beginning to get on her nerves, and headed out of the door.

Gemma watched people on the tube, as they got on, got off, talked, or just stared into space. Some fidgeted, used their phones to scroll, to numb themselves, and some read. Some were happy, some were manic, some were paranoid. She often wondered where the line was, really. If these people were in a secure unit, they would be considered problematic, needing medication. Out here, that was normal. What made the difference? Gemma shook her head, dismissing the thought. If the great psychiatrists couldn't answer it then she certainly could not. She was a nurse. Her job was to care for people.

And somehow, inexplicably, the Woman in White had become part of her job. She needed to help her. She needed to be the one who cared.

Gemma looked out of the window, seeing concrete tunnels, some signs, and the endless dark. The Underground was practical but it was not a picturesque spot. Would Emily have spent much time underground? Where did they go when the bombs came? Did they gather in tube stations? It would make sense. She could have been here. She could have been sitting somewhere here. She touched the window with a fingertip, imagining the windows dripping with water, as the ghost turned up, making her presence known. But she did not come. She was rooted, living out her last days over and over again, in the place that killed her.

Was that insanity? Or was it just how they all did things? So then where was the line?

Gemma shook herself out of her reverie, seeing her stop arriving. She stepped out of the station in a flood of people, some going underground, some emerging like her. Hardly any stopped to consider the transition, the coming into the light. They were focused on where they were going. What they needed to do.

That was what she needed to do. She needed to focus. Crossing the road, she approached the hospital. Her friend met her at the door with a huge smile. They hadn't caught up in ages, largely thanks to work schedules, but she responded right away when Gemma reached out. She should probably reach out to people more often.

Lynn reached out and hugged her, then stepped back, looking her over. "It's nice to see you! What brings you here? I assume you're not planning to switch careers?"

Gemma smiled. "Not really. I was looking into a situation and I needed somebody who actually knows to talk me through it. It's a historical case, of a woman who drowned her three children. Could she have been depressed?"

Lynn raised her eyebrows. "How old were the children?"

"Four, two, and an infant, who died at birth."

Lynn looked up and around at the street. "Come on," she said. "I'll treat you to some coffee in the cafeteria. This isn't something people take well out of context, as a rule, but I think I have your answers."

She turned and headed for the lift, her footsteps silent in the rubber shoes that she wore. She wore her nurse uniform like a second skin, Gemma realised; it was her persona, it was the way she expressed herself. Maternity nurses were jollier, more caring, perhaps, than the Mental Health ones. They always had to use their uniform as a barrier, sometimes a shield. She was pushing people away the whole time, and then by the time she got home it was second nature. Maternity nurses did the opposite. They connected. They reached out. They were the ones you turned to. Just as she was doing right now.

Lynn led and Gemma followed, as Lynn talked lightly of shifts and promotions and how to fit in life into the gaps. She had been dating, she said, but it wasn't going well. She smiled again, and sympathised. She couldn't talk. She was hardly the guru on that. With some prompting, she mentioned her new place, and that her job was going well at the hospital. She did not mention the ghost.

The cafeteria felt vast, an entirely open space with metal cabinets in the middle and two solitary tills. They collected their purchases on laminated wooden trays, smoothly navigating the system. It was as if hospital cafeterias were cloned and placed into hospitals, all the same layout, the same food, with the same staff and the same phrases.

It wasn't difficult to find an empty table far from everyone else. Gemma opened her cup, eyeing the steaming black coffee inside. Perhaps it was better to leave the lid on. Then she couldn't see if it came to life like all the other water did nowadays. She pushed the lid back on, tightly. It was back to an innocuous cup. She could ignore what was boiling inside.

Lynn looked at her from over the table, her expression assessing. "I have to ask, Gemma. I know you said it's a historical case, and I believe you. But are you, or anyone you know, possibly suffering from this? Is that what sparked your research?"

Gemma thought for a moment about her own friend, growing tentatively with her baby, worrying herself sick about everything. "No. I do know someone who is pregnant and stressed, but I don't think she's depressed. She can't get this, can she? From stress?"

Lynn shook her head. "Not usually. There is antenatal depression, which would be flagged by the midwives. I mean, we're overworked, we see too many people, but we do ask the questions. Stress is hard on the mother, hard on the pregnancy, but it doesn't affect them like this does."

She took a sip of her coffee. "You'll know better the differences between psychosis and neurosis than me, and this is what we're talking about here. We're talking about the difference between the brakes failing on a car, or the car really needing a decent tune-up because it's limping its way from A to B.

Post-natal depression is debilitating, of course, and it can be very dangerous. Women do commit suicide from it, but thankfully that doesn't happen a lot. And we do tend to catch most of them as we have a lot of screening questions. But post-natal psychosis, that one is hard to catch. We say that it is rare, but I suspect it isn't. We rely on the mother to tell us if there is a problem, but they wouldn't necessarily know there was a problem, not if they're hallucinating. And the vast majority of women with post-natal psychosis do not kill, I must stress that. But some do."

Gemma leaned forward. "Do we know why they kill their children? Are they aware of what they are doing? Do they get a murderous rage?" She paused, considering. "I just need to know what the motivation is. Is it trauma? Are they deep down, a psychopath?"

Frowning, Lynn nursed her drink for a moment. "It's difficult to say, honestly. I haven't seen that many women with it, they normally go to a secure mother and baby unit. But from what I know, they overwhelmingly kill the kids to save them."

"But save them from what?"

Lynn shrugged. "The devil, or demons. Something's coming for the babies, usually whatever it is they are hallucinating about, and they kill the kids to send them to God. To get them safe. Some mothers hallucinate different faces on their babies and think they are demons, too. I think they don't tend to kill those babies, though. They probably neglect them instead.

But I'm just theorising here. I can see if you can speak directly to some secure unit nurses, if you think it would help -"

"No, no. It's purely out of interest, from a case that I found." Gemma hesitated. "It's a case from 1940, and the woman was convicted of murder. Triple murder. She killed her two older children, as I said, and a baby. The court case mentioned a baby farm, somewhere she went to give birth and they took the baby. Later they killed it. She may not have known. I think that she was raped. I think that the baby was a product of that rape."

Lynn sat for a moment, quite still, as the light from the windows bathed her head in a golden light. She looked quite beautiful, statuesque. Gemma waited, and thought about Emily. Did she kill her children to protect them? If she was hallucinating, and thought her children were in danger, it would have been classic post-natal psychosis. And carrying a baby from a rape, that would destroy anyone's sanity. What if Emily was who she was from grief?

It made so much sense. If the world you lived in was so dangerous, then of course you would kill to liberate the ones you had to protect. But Emily was hunting her. She had said so. And that did not fit. She was not a danger to anyone. Why would she hunt her?

At last, Lynn sighed, her face sad. "I think that something like that would damage someone's mental health so severely, carrying a child from an attack like that, that it would not even have to be post-natal psychosis. I would expect that the trauma would cause problems even before it was born. The poor woman." Lynn sighed, and put her hands on the table. "What happened to the woman? How old was she?"

Gemma felt tears prick her eyes. "She was hanged in prison. She was twenty-five."

Lynn winced. "Oh, terrible. I hope she never realised what she did. When the women come out of the hallucinations, and realise that they murdered their own children, that's the worst point for them. If she died feeling justified, well. I know that's not a correct professional viewpoint, but as a maternity nurse I am here for the mother first, then the baby. I would never wish that agony on anyone."

She tilted her head and frowned. "You said a historical case, and you seem to know a lot about it. What's going on, Gemma?"

That was the question she did not want. She rose hastily, still smiling. "I'm not sure yet. Some strange things are happening. But you have been helpful. I need to go. I'll message soon?"

Gemma meant to be emphatic, but it came out pleading, with hope. Lynn nodded, and let it go. "You know where I am, Gemma. Don't be a stranger."

The words echoed as she left, her footsteps echoing in the halls of the modern building even though the floor was one of those clever linoleum types that was supposed to swallow everything up. The sound burrowed into her brain, leaving those traces that lent themselves to marks in the brain, beats, that you could hang ideas on. Emily wasn't a killer. She wasn't hunting her. She was grieving. And Emily had more to tell her. She had to go home. She had to go home and find out what the ghost needed to say.

THE MEDIUM
RETURNS

G emma waited for the Clairvoyant impatiently, hovering at the door. Her curiosity was at fever pitch, she was desperate to know more about Emily, about her story. Gemma knew there was something they did not know. Something that the court did not know. It was clear that Emily just needed someone to absolve her, someone to understand.

Her rational mind pinched her hard, reminding her that it was easy to fall head first into myths, that finding humanity in something that torments you doesn't make them good, but Gemma was adamant. Her gut always knew best.

Thankfully, Ben was at work, and it would just be Wes with the medium. Ben had not said anything else, but something had shifted. He was her friend, of course, but Gemma wasn't sure if she wanted him there to protect her. She wasn't sure if she even needed protecting anymore.

Wes arrived first, giving her a swift hug, examining her with tight eyes. They were all feeling the tension, the worry. Wes was scared, certainly. She could feel the tension thrumming in his arms and back as if it were a drum vibrating.

Yet he smiled, even though it didn't reach his eyes, and squeezed her arm. Wes was there for her, like always. "Have you seen her again?"

Gemma didn't need to ask who 'her' was. There was only one 'her' that they all thought about. The ghost. "She hasn't spoken to me since she showed me the scene of the attack. She's come again, nightly, but she doesn't look at me. She watches the door, or stands in the corner. I'm not sure what's happening. I really want to talk to her, and get her side. I'm sure she's trying to tell me something. I don't know, but I think she's trying to protect me. Which doesn't make sense as last time, she said she was hunting me. I don't know. I just don't know, but my gut says that there's something I'm missing here."

Wes watched his friend with worried eyes. He turned to the woman, who stood just behind him, this time wearing a scarf and a jacket. Her hair was tied back as before, and she looked calm. Clearly the last experience hadn't caused her any lasting stress. "We can hold a séance, if you prefer," Julie said. "It's not ideal with just the three of us but as the ghost is so present, it might work. We would have to make sure we are not disturbed, though."

Gemma and Wes looked at each other. Wes shrugged. "I don't care how we do this. The fact that we are even communicating with a ghost makes my head boggle. If we hold hands and call her up, all good. Just don't let her eat me."

Gemma's face twitched, just a little. His humour was as ever, badly placed, but she appreciated it. "Deal," she replied. "Shall we do it here?"

The woman agreed, taking her bag out and setting up the small table. She placed candles on either end, the pendulum she used last time, and lit the candles. Tentatively, Gemma approached the table. She had never seen a séance before, and wasn't sure what to expect. Looking at Wes' expression, he didn't know either. They sat down carefully, perched on the edge of the sofa as if they were visiting a distant relative. Julie paid no attention, kneeling down on a cushion and whispering some words that she couldn't catch.

She picked up the pendulum, and then looked at them both. "I will be the conduit for the ghost to speak. You two will need to focus and build the energy so I can concentrate. When she has arrived, you can ask her questions. Yes-no questions are usually best, because there may not be much time. Please, let's link hands and meditate."

Gemma reached out, taking Wes and then Julie's hand, shutting her eyes. She didn't think she could meditate, but she had to do what she could. She concentrated hard on the image that Emily had shown her last time, the beautiful golden river. She was sure that was Emily's safe place, where she could be found. Faintly, Gemma could hear the woman speaking, but it was indistinct, hard to understand.

The medium's voice grew louder. "We are here for the purpose of contacting Emily, the spirit who has been visiting here. We do not wish to speak to anyone else, and we have a circle of protection for ours and for your safety. We are here to speak to Emily. Are you here?"

They waited. Gemma realised she was holding her breath, so intent on listening. There was no response.

Julie spoke again. "We are here to contact the spirit of Emily, who has been visiting here. Gemma is here to speak with you, Emily. Are you here?"

The air crackled around her head, like electricity, and she felt her hair rise. The room went cold and she could hear the rushing of taps. Wes was praying under his breath and his grip tightened. She squeezed his hand hard.

Julie spoke again, but this time her voice was deeper, and strange. "I am Emily."

Gemma swallowed, then took a deep breath. "Emily, I am Gemma. Are you the spirit who has been contacting me?"

"Yes."

The electricity around her head intensified. She was sure by now that her hair was standing on end from the static in the air. She did not dare open her eyes. Her lips were dry. She licked them, and swallowed again.
"Are you hunting me, Emily?"

"No."

Tears found their way from under her closed eyelids as she sagged with relief. She knew it! "Who are you hunting, Emily?"

There was silence. Damn it. Julie had said stick to yes and no questions. She thought for a moment. "Am I in danger, Emily?"

"Yes."

Wes gasped and clutched her hand harder. Gemma didn't respond. The fear returned and brought more with it.
"Am I in danger from a ghost?"

"No."

That made it even worse. Wes spoke, his voice shaking and gruff. "Can you help her, Emily? She's my friend. I can't lose her." He choked back a sob. Gemma started to cry too, the tears falling freely. She concentrated on the warmth of Wes's hand, of Julie's hand. It was something solid, something real.

"Yes. Gemma. Yes."

The candles blew out, and a gust of wind flew through the room. Gemma opened her eyes wide, but there was nothing there. Julie returned to herself, and smiled. "You did well. I hope that was productive."

Wes was still shaking, his face white as a sheet. Tears glistened on his face. "What now, Gem?"

Gemma knew exactly what to do. "The pub. I need a drink. Preferably two."

Wes ordered beer, wine, and two whisky chasers, opting to bring them two at a time as his hands were still shaking. He didn't say anything for a moment, his eyes on the table, as his trembling lips sipped the whisky. Gemma didn't move to take the drink, yet, even though she wanted it. She needed a clear head to process what she had heard. She wished she had taken her phone out to record it. But hearing that creepy voice again, no. No thanks.

"Well, we have established that the ghost isn't trying to kill me with her swamp witch routine. That's something at least. I suppose."

Wes laughed in a maniacal fashion, a shrill shriek leaving his lips. He hastily took another sip, wincing as the drink hit his throat. "God, that stuff is nasty."

Gemma curled her fingers around the tiny glass. She paused, thinking, for a moment. Wes eyed her, his face still grimacing. "You just communicated with a ghost, and it told you you're in danger, but you've not even touched the fire-water. Are you actually mad?"

She laughed, probably because she was expected to, rather than because she actually felt amused. She was numb. "I'm just thinking. It's almost a relief to hear that I'm in danger. And I can't work out why."

Wes frowned and finished off his drink. He shuddered and shut his eyes for a moment. "Ugh."

Gemma pulled the drink towards her and drank it in one deft movement. The spirit burned on its way down, warming her from the inside. She put the glass down firmly on the table. Wes lifted his beer glass in salute. "Well done. You and Zo have always been more manly than me."

Who was hunting her? Her hand went back to her empty wrist, to the spot where her bracelet should be. A cold finger of fear reached in and touched her. She looked up, and met Wes' gaze. "What is it? What have you thought of?"

"I keep losing things, Wes. It's been happening on and off for a couple of years. I never used to be like that, so disorganised. And everyone put it down to the breakdown, that I stayed broken. But I lost my dad's bracelet three days ago. I only take it off at night."

"You think it's been stolen."

It wasn't a question. Wes had a talent of hitting on the right answer, every time, without dancing around the subject. "Yes, I do."

"And if you had the bracelet stolen, that means someone was inside your house." He lifted his phone. "I'm going to call Ben."

Gemma put her hand out to stop him. "No, no. It can't be him, and I don't want him involved. It's been happening for ages, even before I moved in with my dad. And I had the letters, too. I don't know if Zoe ever told you."

His face darkened. "What letters?"

Gemma shivered. It wasn't a subject she liked to re-visit. "I got letters from someone, telling me that they loved me, that they were waiting for me. And then they got creepy, telling me about what I had been doing, warning me off people. I got really frightened and left my place. And then Dad got a letter for me. That was just before I moved in here."

"Someone's stalking you, then."

"I guess so."

"That must be who the ghost was referring to. At least you've got a swamp witch on your side. If I was being stalked I'd probably get Grampa Joe with his false teeth and flatulence."

Gemma shook her head and drank deeply from her wine. She did have Emily on her side. That had to count for something. Her fingers itched to call her dad, but she didn't want him to come over and stay. What if the stalker hurt him, too?

"Why don't you want to tell Ben?"

Wes was his usual observant self, as ever. Gemma shook her head. "I don't know. He's got strange lately, almost as if he thinks we're going to become some-thing. It's not even like I have headspace for that right now, but I don't see Ben like that. He's a nice guy and all, but you know. Not for me."

Wes nodded. "It might be best to switch the guard around, then. I can stay for a bit. And we need to call the police about the stalking. I know, I know," he said as Gemma shook her head. "I know you have no faith in the police. But sometimes you have to get the right people in for the job. Even if they do nothing, it's on record. They know that you've reported a problem. They can't help you if they don't know. And I know you're all up in the air about this ghost thing but it's a poor thing to rely on. What's she going to do, run through him?"

"She's killed prison officers before. You said so yourself. Maybe she is dangerous."

"Hmm. True. I need to call Barnes about that, actually. See if he found out more about the men who died."

Wes put his hands in his pockets, then his jacket, and grimaced. "I must have left it at home. I'll catch him later." Wes looked meaningfully at Gemma. "And I want to file a report on this. I can even do it online for you, on your behalf. Please?"

"Fine." The word came out in a rush, of giving in, letting go. This was bigger than herself. Gemma did need to do things properly, even if the police would do nothing anyway. She drank the rest of her drink in silence, thinking.

Wes watched her. "We're here for you, you know. Zo has been reading and researching about ghosts and how to remove them, and was ready to do an exorcism. Obviously, I'll tell her what happened today, so she knows that the ghost isn't after you. She'll be relieved. And why don't you come over tomorrow for tea?" He smiled. "Just us three. I'll cook something nice."

That did sound good. Gemma smiled and agreed, feeling relief flood through her. She had a stalker, and a ghost who was haunting her, flooding her apartment at night. But she had friends. She wasn't going to go down without a fight.

GEMMA: THE FINAL SHOWDOWN

She turned the key quietly in the lock and stepped in. It was cool, and dark. That was odd. Normally the timers were switched on by now. Gemma took her coat off, listening. The place felt empty. She would make the most of it, and try and make a plan. Preferably with all the lights on, and music. She stepped into her living room and froze. There was a dark shape sitting on the sofa.

"Ben! You scared me! Why are you sitting in the dark?"

He did not reply for a moment. Gemma hovered, waiting, feeling suspiciously as if it was his house, that she had walked in, and was about to be told off for something. The tension was so thick that you could cut it with a knife.

"I'm quite upset, Gem. After all that I've done, and then you go and tell Wes that I'm not the one for you. I think that's quite rude. You could have told me, first. I think I'm owed that."

Ben looked up, his face sinister in the shadow. "Is there someone else? Is that it? Have you betrayed me?"

"What? Ben, I don't know what you're talking about. How do you know what I said to Wes, anyway, and how is it even your business?"

He smiled, a cold, angry smile. His eyes glinted. This didn't look like the usual Ben. "He texted me when you were at the pub. He told me everything. That you were drinking and talking about me being not for you. Ditching me. Making plans without me. Replacing me with him."

Gemma shifted her feet, wishing she hadn't put her keys away. This was starting to look dangerous. "We aren't together, Ben. We're friends. Or were, considering how you are behaving. I would like you to leave."

Her tone was firm, as if he were one of her patients, using the tone that the other staff knew was a warning of a possible incident, coming over to offer support and back-up. But Gemma was alone, and this person looked more and more like a stranger. In her house. He was in her house.
Ben stood, rising slowly in a fluid movement. He did not take his eyes from her face. "I really wish you hadn't said that, Gem."

Gemma stood back, feeling the thread of fear winding again around her heart. "What's going on, Ben? Why are you here?"

She looked at her wrist. "Did you take my bracelet, Ben?"

He didn't speak.

Gemma thought of that afternoon, of Wes mentioning he would call Barnes. But he didn't. "Wes didn't have his phone with him, Ben. He didn't text you. How did you know what I said?"

Ben took a step around the table, casually. "I've done so much for you, Gem. I've waited so long for you. I promised that I would wait, until you were ready. I've protected you all this time. And now, you betray me. I wonder if I was wrong. I wonder if you are like all the others."

Gemma turned for the door, her instincts telling her to get out, fast. Ben grabbed her left wrist, his fingers vice-like. They were cold. "Not so fast, Gem. You've got some apologising to do."

Her head turned slowly, looking at his cold, flat eyes. How had he hidden this side? How long had he been watching?

"How long have you been watching me?"

He didn't answer. It was as if he hadn't heard. Gemma was just a puppet in his tapestry, the fool that was caught in his net. Ben turned away, whispering to himself, still holding onto her wrist.

Her head started to spin. The letters. The letters. Ben knew she moved to her dad's house. The things disappearing. Even when he began staying there, he never asked where anything was. Ben was the stalker. Ben was the stalker.

She pulled at her wrist, hard. "Let me go, Ben. Just let me go. Leave my house, and don't look back. And nobody needs to know about this."

The lies fell from her mouth. There was no way she was letting him get away with it. But Gemma would say whatever she had to get away. Survival at all costs, was the motto on her wards. Do what you had to do to get to safety.

Ben was tall, but slight. Gemma could probably knock him to the floor with ease, if he was caught by surprise. But he was just out of reach. She moved closer. If she could hit him with a lamp, maybe...

He turned back, his eyes black pools of ink, filled with hate and rage. This was not going to be pretty at all. Gemma braced herself, and shoved at him as hard as she could with her right shoulder. Ben staggered, stepping back, and his grip loosened on her wrist. That was all she needed. She got the table between them, running for the kitchen. If she could get a knife, maybe, or something – she grabbed the biggest knife from the block and faced him, the stranger who now blocked her way, his grin widening.

Taps at her back began to rush, the water boiling hot. She could hear the ferocious snarl of the water, the thud of it hitting the sink. Even as her hair stood on end, and water rose, flooding the room, Gemma started to breathe, hard. Emily was coming. She was coming.

"Emily!" she shouted, at the top of her voice. "Emily!"

And Emily came.

Rising head first from the dark boiling water that filled the room, she emerged, her hair lank, clinging to her face, her dress white. She turned her head, slowly, and her mouth opened. Her eyes were sunken, dark, and terrifying. As the ghost moved her head she shuddered, moving as if she were a part of one of those stop-frame films, stepping forward in a robotic fashion. Ben's eyes were wide, his mouth hanging open.

The ghost drew nearer, her mouth moving as if she were speaking, pointing right at Ben. Her fingers were bony, white in places where the bones poked through. Water dripped from her garments, re-joining the flood of water.

"YOU!"

"YOU! HUNTING YOU. COMING FOR YOU!"

The words flew out of the ghost's mouth, hanging in the air, getting louder and louder. Her voice was terrible, with the resonance of a group of church bells, ringing hard in Gemma's ears. It hurt. She wanted to cover her ears, block out the sound, but she didn't dare to move. Her hands were frozen in place. Then Ben moved, as fast as a snake, and grabbed her again, pulling Gemma to him, using her as a shield.

"I'll kill her, demon! I'll kill her!" Ben's voice was raspy as he shrieked, his breath was coming out in pants. Gemma struggled, then tried to fall against him, push him down. But he had learned quickly and was ready for her.

"Look at what you've done, Gem," he hissed. "If you had just been sensible, and not run from me, none of this would have happened. You are the cause of it. You. You made me do this. You made me angry!"

Gemma screamed as loud as she could. "Help! Help me! Someone help me!"

The ghost drew nearer, ignoring Gemma, her eyes on Ben. "YOU WILL DIE. DIE. DIE."

Ben had hold of Gemma's arm, drawing the knife nearer to her throat. She struggled, pushing as hard as she could, but slowly the knife made its ascent. Gemma locked eyes with the ghost, pleading, but the ghost did not pause. It looked away, focused on its target. Hot tears fell from Gemma's eyes.

There was banging, banging, something large hitting the front door, hard. At last the door opened, with two figures rushing in, their faces red, out of breath.

Gemma screamed, "Be careful! He's dangerous! Wes, it was -"

Ben cut off her words, pulling the knife closer to her throat. "Don't come closer! I'm going to kill this whore! Get back!"

Zoe moved nearer, her expression carved in stone. "Give it up, Ben. We already called the police. It's over."

Ben paused. "You're lying."

Zoe shook her head. "I'm not." She looked straight at Gemma. "Barnes rang us. He said that all of the officers Emily attacked, were corrupt officers. Some were hurting the female prisoners. Emily was hunting the bad ones down, not the good ones. He warned you that she was probably protecting you, not hurting you. We already knew that, so we called the police and told them about the stalker.

Then, all the taps in our house went off, and then the damn sprinkler outside. Everything. We knew it was the ghost. She was warning us. We ran out and drove here as fast as we could. I called the police again and told them you're in danger right now. They'll be here any minute, I was on the phone when the dispatch person heard you scream from outside the apartment."

Zoe's face started to crumple. "I'm sorry we didn't get here sooner. We drove as fast as we could. It's going to be okay."

Gemma was so focused on Zoe's words that for a moment she didn't register that Wes was gone from by Zoe's side. She blinked, processing it, before seeing a dark shape hurtling towards her left side from the other entrance to her bedroom. He barrelled into Ben, knocking him to the floor, hitting him as hard as he could.

She took the chance, running to Zoe, and holding her tight.
"Get out!" Wes shouted from the kitchen, and Zoe pulled her hard. "Come on!"

Gemma turned to run, but stopped for a moment to look at the ghost. Already the water was subsiding and she was sinking back into the floor. The ghost nodded just once before she disappeared. Zoe pulled on her hand again. "Quickly!"

Gemma moved, following her friend. "I'm sorry. I just wanted to say thank you to Emily. She saved me."

Zoe looked back, and then shook her head. "I didn't see a thing. But I'll thank her too." Zoe reached out and grabbed her friend, hugging her fiercely. "Damnation, I thought I'd lost you! Don't you do that to me again."

There was more commotion inside, so they rushed out, running down the flights of stairs. Doors were opening on the lower floors, heads poking out. They paid them no heed as they ran, seeing men running up the stairs, women remaining to gawk. Gemma could hear sirens in the distance, getting louder. It sounded like Wes and Zo really had got the cavalry on the way. Tears started to fall again as she ran, her friend at her side.

They skidded out of the door, just as the first police car was in sight, siren blazing. Another followed in the near distance. Zoe clutched Gemma again. "You're staying with us tonight. They'll probably want to examine your flat or something."

Gemma wasn't sure if they would, but she wasn't arguing. "You said that you knew the ghost was trying to warn you when all the taps went off. How did you know?"

Zoe shrugged, looking sheepish. "Well, I can't say I did really know. The taps went off, and I started screaming and shouting for Wes, and he came running in shouting about what was going on, and then we both thought of you, and ran out of the door. Half of me thought you two were wrong about the ghost and she was drowning you or something and it was actually your ghost turning on the taps to tell me."

She drew back and fixed Gemma with a hard look. "And you had better do that if ever you die. You come back as a ghost and let me know first. You hear?"

Gemma laughed and agreed. "Deal. What happened next?"

"Well, the rest you know, really. We got here, and you were screaming, and Wes was banging on the door and trying to open it like the police do in films. He's going to have a bruised shoulder tomorrow, put it that way. I had the key so I opened it the normal way, and there you were, with Ben trying to murder you. As I said, I was on the phone to 999, and they stepped it all up when they heard your shouts. And that was that, the rest you know. But Ben -"

Zoe paused, rubbing her forehead with her hand. "I did not see that coming. I would never have thought Ben was the stalker. If I had known, I-"

Gemma shushed her, pulling Zoe in for a hug. "None of us knew. It's not our fault. I spent hours with him in that apartment and didn't spot a thing. There's no point worrying about it now."

Police ran past them, standing by the entrance, as they poured into the building. Gemma looked up at the cloudy sky, wondering what on earth she would do next. What on earth she was supposed to feel.

"I am exhausted." Zoe looked it, too, her eyes showing shadows, her shoulders wilting. The house echoed
with the voices of officers in uniform, of Zoe running
about making tea for all and sundry, of questions being
asked over and over again.

Wes stepped over and put his arm around Zoe. "You
did great. You saved your mate, talked down a bad guy,
AND kept the entire local constabulary in tea. All I did
was try and open a door, which you then opened, with
the key." He laughed and kissed her on the cheek. "You
can be Super-Mum and I'll be Robin."

Gemma smiled, watching the two of them together.
They had something special. Wes looked over and
smiled back. His eyes were bleary. "At least it's done."

Zoe sat down next to her, and stroked her arm gently.
"It will take time. We're here for you."

There was a lot of meaning in those few words. Gemma
was grateful for them, and to the pair who had done
so much. "I keep thinking about it, when the cops
took Ben away in handcuffs. It doesn't feel real. I keep
thinking he's going to just walk right in that door."

Zoe shuddered. "No, that's not going to happen. From
what that policeman said, Ben is going to prison for a
long time. Not only did he try to kill you, but they think
he's done this before. If he admits to it, well, I don't
know how long he'll get, but I hope he gets a long time.
Right, Wes?"

Wes shifted, thinking. "Maybe. It depends. Attempted
murder is the bigger sentence, but you don't need to
worry about that. Not right now."

Gemma shook her head. "I'm not going to think about it. But I am going to go to bed." She leaned to kiss Zoe on the forehead, and then got up, hugging Wes hard. "I love you guys. Thanks for saving me." The words came out a little garbled, her voice shaking, but Wes's arms tightened around her as he replied. "That's what we do, Gem. Always."

She collapsed into the spare bed, utterly spent. The lamp gleamed a warm, soft light, and her hot cocoa sat just beside her on the tiny bedside table. It felt cosy. Safe. Her eyes were heavy, but Gemma wondered if she would ever be able to sleep. Would Emily come back? She peeped over the edge, looking at the floor. But no water rose up from the carpet, and no ghost appeared. Gemma sighed. It was silly to expect that it would, really. She wrapped herself in the blanket, sinking immediately into sleep.

Gemma dreamed of a river cast in golden light, that stretched out as far as she could see. The buildings were strange, mishappen, as if something had bitten and torn them up. The river twinkled in the sun, calling to her. Walking closer, she bent and touched the water gently. It was warm to the touch.

Straightening, she looked around for Emily. She had called her here, Gemma was sure of it.

She looked up and down the bank, and across the river. And then she saw a glint of light and Emily came, dressed in white, her hair flowing. The ghost beckoned for her to follow, and so she did. They walked along the bank until the ghost paused and looked out. Her face looked solemn. Gemma followed her gaze.

There was an image of Emily, holding her two children, standing in the water. They were asleep, cradled against her chest. Emily was speaking to the sky, and then slowly let her children slip away. Gemma watched the scene, and she cried.

"Did you kill them to save them?"

The ghost turned to her, a solitary tear on her face. She nodded, once. "I was afraid," Emily whispered. "I was afraid that they were being hunted. I understand better now. But I hope that they went to God, and are happy there, despite what I did. One day, I hope to see them again. If God says that I can."

Gemma began to cry, great weeping sobs that racked her body. Was she crying for the babies, or Emily, or herself? She supposed it was for them all. "What were their names?"

The ghost looked back at the water, as the scene in the river began again. The light struck the little boy's face as he snuggled against her. "My son is Eddie. My daughter is called Betty."

Gemma stepped closer, and without thinking, she put her arm around the ghost's waist. "They're beautiful," she whispered hoarsely. "I'm sorry about what happened to you, Emily. I'm so sorry."

They stood there together, as Gemma cried, and Emily looked out at the river in the setting sun.

THE WOMAN IN WHITE HUNTS

The new prisoner was screaming again. Pete checked his watch and then looked over at the suicide watch file. "Is the new one on 15 minute obs yet?"

"Not yet. But I think he will be, soon. He sounds pretty unstable. He keeps screaming about something coming to get him."

"It doesn't sound like he'll make it to trial, then. Do you think he's going to go for the insanity route?"

Brian shrugged. "Maybe. I don't see that it's better than here but each to their own, eh. We've got twenty minutes till we do the rounds. Coffee?"

Pete nodded. The man never usually offered – he may as well make the most of it.

The man shook and screamed in the corner of his cell, his whole body shaking with fear. Tears ran down his face and his hands were bloodied from hitting the walls over and over again.

The cell went cold and water began to seep in from outside the door, slowly rising. The water was dark and dank. The puddle of water stretched, touching the prisoner tauntingly, then flowing with a rush as the cell began to fill. The water was up to his waist. Shrieking, the man scrambled to his feet, his back against the wall.

Ben's eyes were wide, bloodshot, and terrified.

And they were fixed on the shape that slowly rose from the middle of the water, the hair dripping, the eyes black pits of rage. The creature was dressed in a white dress that flowed into the inky water. It raised a hand that was part bone, and part rotting skin. It pointed at Ben.

"YOU!"

He heard the word reverberate in his skull, circling and drumming within his brain. He screamed at the pain of it, as the terror made his blood pulse in his straining veins. The water rose higher. It was at Ben's chest, freezing his limbs, holding him in place. The ghost came nearer, her desiccated face almost touching his own. The eye sockets were dark, empty, and cold. Cold hands came up and grabbed him by the throat, lifting him up, squeezing mercilessly.

He tried to scream, but the hands were a vice around his throat, and all that came out was a tortured rasp.

The ghost tilted its head and regarded Ben as he struggled for air, his face becoming mottled. His feet kicked hard, then feebly, as he slowly lost the fight. As his eyes closed, the ghost lowered him into the water, letting him slip underneath the oily black surface.

The ghost turned, with a satisfied smile on her withered face. Walking through the prison door, she turned and looked back in through the tiny window, a skeletal face with staring black eyes. The water disappeared, leaving the body lying dead on the floor.

Outside the cell, the Woman in White turned and surveyed her new home. She smiled, and disappeared.

COMING BACK

S he had meant to come back for a long time, but excuses had set in, or she was busy, or things happened, or she didn't know what to say.

As Gemma stepped up to the river, she knew that it just hadn't been time yet. That now, at last, it was.

Gemma did not know why, or how, but she knew that it was this river, this very one, that Emily had come to in her last days. It felt like the one she saw in the dreams. Gemma drew close to the bank and listened to the gentle water bubbling and gurgling, of the small tide lapping at the edge.

The light warmed as the sun set, and bathed the river with a golden light. It was time. Gemma took a deep breath, feeling her daughter stir sleepily against her chest, then subside. Gemma tightened her arms around her, held her baby close. Her hand went to her wrist, and touched the bracelet that she never removed. It never would now it was returned to her.

"Hello, Emily. I know I haven't been back in a long while. I've had things to do, things to make sense of. But I did, and I got safe, and I built myself a life. But I never came back to thank you for saving me, and I am sorry for that. I should have. I just didn't know what to say."

Tears fell from Gemma's eyes as she paused for a moment. "I had a little girl, a few months ago. I met a nice man. I think he's nice, I mean you never know, nowadays, but he seems good. And we had a baby. She's here. I wanted you to meet her. I wanted to tell you her name. I decided to name her after the bravest woman I know. I called her Emily."

There was no answer but the rippling of the river, and the warm embrace of the sunset as it bathed the river with warm light. But Gemma knew that Emily had heard. As she walked away, tears still falling, she held her baby tightly, knowing that her life might not be perfect, but it was going to be okay. It was going to be okay.

AUTHOR'S NOTE

E mily's story is a tragic one, but not that out of the ordinary when considering the time. Most of her story is historically accurate, but in terms of the baby farming, the last baby farmer was convicted and hanged in 1907, not 1940.

However, women were still hanged for murder in 1940 in the UK, although not for infanticide if the child was under one year old. Clearly, even our 20th century counterparts understood that post-natal depression and post-natal psychosis were a very big deal. There were abortions, just as described in this story, which were considered to be legal as long as it was taking place before what they called the quickening.

The bombing in London did not start until September of 1940 and much of the year was spent waiting for the bombs to fall. Young women worked for the ARP, delivering messages about raids. They usually travelled by bikes or roller skates, as they were more practical in a bomb-torn city, just as they did in this story.

Holloway Prison hanged women prisoners up until 1955, which was the last time a woman was hanged in the UK. So our fictional character, Emily, would have been taken there for her last sad days. Interestingly, at the time of writing this, Holloway has been closed and a number of new properties are being built on the site. If the place becomes haunted by a vengeful lady ghost then I will simply raise my eyebrow and deny all knowledge. Life sometimes does imitate art.

The Woman in White as a myth does exist in Hungarian stories, but we do have a ton of White Lady ghosts running around in England who seem to cause trouble popping up and frightening people half to death. Most originated in tragedy, just as Ben said.

There are many urban myths about prisons being haunted, and several officers have seen a ghost from time to time. Whether they have, or it's merely a trick of the light, I do not know. But I can tell you that there is a lot of sadness in those places, just as Barnes said.

I spent many years teaching in prisons: some of Emily's tale was inspired by their stories, the women who are long forgotten. I will not forget them.

E.M. 12.12.2023

ABOUT THE AUTHOR

E ryn is a non genre-specific fiction author who dabbles in writing horror, dystopian and cosy sci-fi, and fantasy. And not to mention that they have been writing poetry for a long time, having published seven poetry collections. They studied History and Psychology at University so particularly enjoyed writing this story with elements of history and mental illness.

Eryn lives in South Germany with their young family and works as an English teacher. When they are not writing or working they are on their bike or finding time in the forest. They love travel and dream of visiting vineyards all over the world. Their favourite things are new socks, cloud watching, cheese and dragons. Hopefully not all together.

Their current projects are folk horror, dystopian and dark retellings of fairy tales, and cosy sci-fi. They are also working on Book Two of the Sovereigns, a dystopian dragon fantasy series.

You can find them in most places online, but Twitter is probably where they hang out most. If you enjoyed the book, let them know! You're welcome to review, too. Authors need those reviews to keep going.

Https://Linktr.ee/Eryn.McConnell

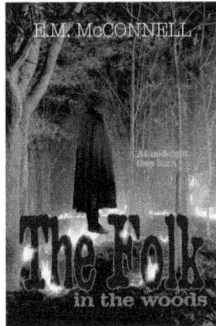

In the beautiful English village of Ravenswood, the annual harvest festival is more than a celebration—it's a renewal of the pact with the earth and the honouring of the ancient story that founded their home.

A group of outsiders arrived, drawn by the village's rustic charm, but they soon realise there is more afoot than meets the eye. The villagers follow strange traditions, and there are cryptic symbols carved into fence posts and doors. As the festival draws nearer, the ancient deity that the village worships awakens, and it is hungry for blood.

The Folk In The Woods will be released 21.07.24.

CONTENT WARNINGS

Reference to rape by two men – fade to black

Trauma and depression

Failed abortion

Thoughts of suicide

Killing own children by means of sedation and drowning -on page, not graphic.

Execution by hanging – fade to black

Stalking

Violence from the ghost – on-page.

Milton Keynes UK
Ingram Content Group UK Ltd.
UKHW011315020524
442122UK00027B/289